He ached to hold her
strength of her heartbeat.

But how could he? She had no idea what they had planned
years ago. And he had no right to tell her, to drop it in her lap
like a too-hot potato. No, he had promised David he would
bide his time and wait. And he would pray she would remember who he was, who she was, what they had been to each
other. And no matter what, he would carry with him forever
the memory of her soft brown eyes staring into his as if she
remembered every vow they had ever made to each other.

Abe's rap at the door interrupted Joshua's misery. Joshua
admitted him, feeling useless as the rangy man bent in sorrow
by his wife's bedside.

Joshua heard Callie explain about the loss, his admiration
for her bravery growing as she did so. It seemed that only a
few moments passed before she joined him at the table. Her
petite oval face was flushed, her eyes fringed with crimson,
clearly a result of her grief. Again Joshua wanted to touch
her, to assure himself that five years of waiting was over.

"I must thank you," Callie said after she settled onto a
chair. She used both hands to smudge away the tears she had
cried as she spoke with Abe.

"It is you who deserves the credit," he replied. He was
amazed at her ability to put aside her pain and attend to those
who needed her compassion. Without thinking, he reached
out and squeezed her hand, suddenly realizing that her reaction would likely be shock.

Callie didn't pull away. She only looked at him with huge
dark eyes. She was the most beautiful woman he had ever
known, but he was sure she viewed him through eyes of
friendship, not love, something he was powerless to change.
After arriving at the mission, he had learned she was expected
to wed Levi. Joshua didn't care for the situation, but he would
not damage what she and Levi had established together.

As if uncomfortable with his gaze, Callie abruptly stood
and went over to the hearth, where she prodded the embers of
the fire. When she turned back, he was gone.

TAMMY SHUTTLESWORTH is a native of Ohio who resides in Louisiana with her husband and two daughters. Though retired from the Air Force, she still works with ROTC classes. Her first book is inspired by the rich Ohio history she grew up hearing and exploring.

A Different Kind of Heaven

Tammy Shuttlesworth

Heartsong Presents

To my mother, Janet Bente,
who always wanted to live "back in those days,"
and to my daughters, Caryn and Taryn,
who are glad they don't.

A note from the author:
I love to hear from my readers! You may correspond with me
by writing: **Tammy Shuttlesworth**
Author Relations
PO Box 719
Uhrichsville, OH 44683

ISBN 1-57748-483-5

A DIFFERENT KIND OF HEAVEN

Cover illustration by Gary Maria.

PRINTED IN THE U.S.A.

one

Callie Troyer watched the woman lying on the handmade wooden bed. Even from across the room she recognized the hopelessness of the situation. If she didn't do something soon, there would be two more graves in "God's Acres," and the Solomon name would again mark them both.

"Child. . .comes. . .too soon!" the young woman screamed, pain twisting her delicate features into a tortured mask.

Callie hurried to Suzannah's bedside, her nerves ready to snap. What could she do? She had already administered every concoction the Delaware tribe's medicine woman—Helping Hands—had taught her how to make before the woman had returned to Pennsylvania. Suzannah was Callie's dearest friend in all the world. But Callie had not known enough to help her the last time Suzannah was with child—she miscarried—and Callie knew no more now than she had then.

Another contraction lanced through Suzannah's body, and she grasped Callie's hand, her white-knuckled fingers digging into flesh. "Make it *stop!*"

The image of two tiny graves, barely nine months old, passed through Callie's mind.

"I am trying, Suzannah," she said, squeezing her eyes shut and praying silently that they both be able to accept whatever happened as God's will.

The door to the log cabin swung open and Callie turned toward the sound, expecting to see Suzannah's husband or mother. What she saw instead left her speechless. A rugged man, cast in handsome silhouette by the evening sun, strode into the room as though he had every right to be there. Finding her voice, Callie moved between the man and Suzannah. "Who are you and why are you here?"

"I have come to help," he replied matter-of-factly. He glanced around the sparsely furnished cabin as if assessing the situation. His gaze settled on Callie.

Lake-blue eyes held her doe-brown ones for a moment. His scrutiny made her uncomfortable, and she quickly looked away. Her gown was worn, threadbare in places, and was wrinkled from her long vigil. To make matters worse, her bonnet hung on a peg near the door. Nervously, she reached up to touch the blond curls that lay across her shoulders, thinking how improper it was for him to see her bare-headed.

But impropriety couldn't be a concern right now. Forgetting the bonnet, Callie swallowed her discomfort and lifted her gaze to his once again. She fixed her hands defiantly on her slender hips. "I do not need your help."

"I–I do," Suzannah gasped behind her.

His face was serious as he crossed the room, his dusty black boots kicking up straw as he walked. He tossed a slouch hat through the air, settling it frighteningly close to a burning taper on the table. Shrugging off a buckskin jacket, he proceeded to dig a gnarled twig out of a large buckskin pouch he carried.

"Take this," he ordered Callie. Against her will, Callie took the twig. "Mash the end," he continued, paying no heed to what Callie thought of the matter. "Mix it in hot water." Authority echoed in the room, and he turned back to hold the other woman's slim wrist in his hand.

Suzannah did not resist him—Callie absorbed that much before she moved to do as he had commanded. *But Suzannah is not herself,* Callie thought. *She is delirious with pain and remembered grief of what happened before.* Callie paused and glanced back at the stranger. Perhaps she should insist he leave. But how? And what if he had the ability to make Suzannah's contractions stop?

Fighting churning emotions, Callie poured hot water from a kettle into a bowl. Her hands shook, but she carefully followed the man's instructions. Grabbing the end of an antler she had used earlier to mix her own remedy, she crushed the twig's bark. A bitter odor wafted up with the steam and she waved a hand at the offensive smell.

"Three minutes," he commanded.

Callie turned to look at him, thinking once again to tell him to leave. He met her gaze squarely, and when she noticed that his somber eyes flickered with warmth and compassion, she held her tongue. That did not diminish her questioning thoughts, though. How had he found them? Schoenbrunn Mission was at least a four-day ride on horseback from Fort Pitt. Strangers simply did not just happen upon the settlers here, and if they did, they were usually traders. He didn't appear to be a trader. So who *was* he?

She looked at the candle's flame dancing in the pale yellow liquid in the bowl and remembered what she was supposed to be doing. He had said three minutes. She must keep track. "One hundred and one, one hundred and two, one hundred and three," she began.

"Quietly. I am praying," he requested softly.

This not only surprised Callie, it unnerved her. But she counted on silently as he transformed from a man of power to a man of prayer. His hair, blacker than his boots and wavy, was creased where his hat had rested. His face was rugged and tanned. All in all, she thought he looked rather arrogant, but a certain charm seemed to be present in his eyes as they appraised her.

Callie felt the warmth of a blush tint her cheeks. What was he looking at? The braid she had not kept up properly on the back of her head? She shook herself. The church had rules about unmarried men and women associating with each other. And she could imagine what Levi would say if he found out she was interested in this stranger. Better to concentrate on the rules than to think about the blueness of his eyes. She mashed and stirred, all the while biting her lower lip.

When the time was up, she came forward hesitantly. "Here." She handed him the bowl, wrinkling her nose at the odor; she was curious to see what he would do with it.

He took the bowl, his large, nimble fingers spanning it easily, and passed it under his nose. He dipped his hand into the liquid. When he raised it, golden drops trickled from his fingers before he smeared them on Suzannah's upper lip.

"What is it?" Callie whispered, forgetting her concerns about him for the moment.

"Just watch."

Mystified, she circled around the end of the bed and sat on the far edge.

"Are you still here, Callie?" Suzannah's words were slurred now, and she looked as if she could not hold her eyes open.

"I am here," she assured, reaching out to pat Suzannah's hand. He glanced at her as if he disapproved. Callie quickly pulled her hand back to her lap.

Silence grew heavy. She had to say something. Why not demand again that he tell her who he was? Bravely she raised her chin to do just that. She had missed her chance. Was he praying? Or sleeping? She couldn't tell, but her curiosity to know him better was overwhelming her good sense.

"The only thing wrong with curiosity is that sometimes the cat does not come home," Ruth Lyons, Suzannah's mother, always said. Surely there was no harm in watching him, though. For a moment.

Dark locks of hair clung to his forehead. There were lines around his eyes and mouth, but they simply added character.

He is probably a Magicworker, she thought. But Magicworker usually meant "black medicine." Somehow, Callie did not think this man had anything to do with witchcraft.

She glanced at the woman who had taken her in five years ago and helped her adjust to the Christian life she now led. Sleep had eased the tension on Suzannah's face, and the worry was gone from her lips. Suzannah's life, and that of her unborn child, did not appear to be in danger.

The stranger had helped Suzannah—something Callie had not been able to do. Callie felt inadequate—and irritated. But the fact that Suzannah was resting, the dark smudges under her eyes already beginning to pale, was more important just now, Callie reminded herself.

Her gaze traveled back to the stranger. His eyes shifted to an icy blue, and she shivered as a tiny dimple at the corner of his mouth caught her attention. She was suddenly undecided about the way he looked.

"Callie?" Suzannah's hands cradled her abdomen tenderly, as if rocking a baby bird to sleep.

Callie scooted toward the head of the bed, aware the gap between her and the mysterious man had closed to inches.

She reached out to hold Suzannah's hand. "I am here."

"So. . .good," Suzannah murmured before her head rolled to one side and she fell asleep.

Callie turned a questioning look his way. She could only hope her expression did not betray the awe she felt for him. He said nothing if it did. He only smiled, a smile that said he was a traveler, a drifter, a man no one would tie down.

"She will be all right." His words filled Callie with the tiniest ray of hope.

It seemed unreasonable, this urge she felt to trust him. She didn't know him. How many times must she remind herself of that? If he were a Magicworker, he would be gone tomorrow, taking with him his knowledge and all the other wonders he had in his bag. Which would leave her here, in the eastern part of what some called "O-he-yo," with no help for Suzannah if this happened again. *If I can get my hands on some of his remedies, it will not matter if he does go,* Callie thought. *I must learn what I can before he disappears.*

"What did you give her?" she asked.

Faint laughter danced in his eyes. "Family secret," he drawled.

"You are not going to tell me?" She was not afraid, only curious, and she wondered why she felt so at ease with a man she didn't know.

He shook his head and a renegade swatch of hair fell across his forehead. He raked it back with his hand.

Callie crossed her arms in front of her. "Why not?"

"Man should never give away his secrets too easily."

"You have others?" She couldn't believe she had asked the question, but there it was, out in the open between them.

A shadow swept across his face. "Every man has things he does not reveal to just anyone." He glanced around the room and wrinkled his nose at the assortment of pouches she had left lying on the table.

"Oh," she said, her eyes tracking his gaze and seeing the piles identifying her attempts to help Suzannah. He just studied the scene, absorbing it, as if it told him everything he needed to know.

"I am not really trained in this sort of thing, you see. . ." she started. He faced her, his jaw tightening as he peered from under dark brows. "But I am the only one we have here who. . .oh, never mind. You do not want to know that."

"Go on. I will listen," he said patiently.

Callie gritted her teeth then went on. "Helping Hands was our local medicine woman. She decided to go back to Pennsylvania, and before she did, I made her tell me whatever she could. It was not enough," she finished in a rush as tears sprang to her eyes. She couldn't help but remember how she had failed nine months ago.

"I see." He turned back to Suzannah.

Callie had other questions she wanted to ask, but her mouth refused to utter them. Why were his boots so dusty? Why were his eyes so blue? How had he happened to find the settlement they had established?

"Life is full of questions, is it not?" He unfolded his legs in front of him and leaned back in the chair.

Callie glanced at Suzannah and was about to deny she had been thinking of asking anything, when he cocked his head toward her friend.

"She will give birth early. Twins."

Air spilled from Callie's lungs and she choked back a gasp. She recovered her composure quickly. "Yes, she did," she said coolly. "Nine months ago. Little girls. We lost them."

He frowned and shook his head, then pointed to the bulge of Suzannah's abdomen. "She is carrying twins now."

Callie had suspected the same thing, but had not told anyone. How did *he* know? She pressed her lips into a thin line.

"You knew, did you not?" he probed.

She could only nod and hope he didn't press her for more information.

"One of them. . ." He pressed his thumb and forefinger to the bridge of his nose, and when he did, his tattered shirt sleeve fell back, revealing a blood-red scar running down his right forearm.

Callie wondered about the injury; it made him seem even more mysterious. But she squared her shoulders and forced the question aside. "What?" Her jaw quivered. "What about one of them?"

"Not now," he mouthed.

He hadn't shut the door all the way, and cool mid-April air penetrated the room. Callie pulled her shawl tighter around her shoulders. She thought about shutting the door but didn't move.

"Shall we pray?" His hand covered hers without permission. It was a rider's hand—strong, callused, but gentle. His words echoed not only in her head but in her heart.

"Dear Lord, we commend this woman and her unborn children into your care. We ask that you watch over them, protect them, hold them in your hands."

Relief flashed through Callie. He was not a Magicworker, then; they didn't believe in God. At least she didn't think they did. His strong tenor floated around her. She could feel herself relaxing.

If they hadn't been praying, she would have jumped up and jerked away from him. After all, she was responsible for Suzannah's health, not him! Besides not knowing what he had given Suzannah, Callie had no idea who he was! She stiffened.

Seemingly in response, he brought the prayer to a close and released her hand. Then he crossed his legs and placed his hands, fingers entwined, on top of his right knee. Callie watched, torn between wanting to ask him to leave and wanting to know about what he had done to help Suzannah.

"Amen," he whispered, drawing her back to reality.

Callie repeated the word. She moistened her lips. Silence fell between them. In the background, Suzannah's even breathing rose and fell. A gentle breeze slipped in through the still-open door. It swirled around Callie's feet, lifting the hem of her long gray skirt.

"Survival belongs to the fit," he said seriously, his brows narrowing, becoming two slashes of brown.

What did he mean by that? She was worn out from sitting, and pacing, and hoping, and from praying that Suzannah's pains would stop.

She motioned toward her friend. "How did you know what to do?"

He leaned forward slightly. "Family—"

"Secret," she interrupted, feeling a tiny thrill of excitement that she could joke with him so easily.

He winked, long-lashed lids momentarily concealing the blue depths from her.

She let out a long breath.

"Someday. . ." His voice faded.

"Someday what?" she challenged. Why did she feel she must banter with him?

"You will see."

She hoped she appeared unruffled. "What if I do not want to see?"

An easy smile played at the corners of his mouth. The dimple she had seen earlier grew deeper. "You will," he promised.

Callie had no doubt she would. But what exactly was it she would see?

two

Joshua watched as Callie busied herself cleaning up the table. The dreary gray dress she wore seemed to drain the color from her face. A bit of tea-colored lace around the neckline and sleeves added just a touch of lightness to her attire, and her boyish frame was accented by an apron tied tightly around her waist. But what held his attention were her eyes, newborn fawn in hue, and no less mesmerizing now than he had found them before. They revealed every emotion Callie felt, whether she wanted them to or not.

As if she sensed him scrutinizing her, Callie wiped her hands on her apron and moved to stand at the foot of Suzannah's bed. She gazed at him for a moment before bluntly asking where he was from.

"Pennsylvania," he replied, giving up only as much as he judged safe for the moment. It hurt, not being able to reveal everything, but intuitively he sensed that doing so would ruin any chance he had with her.

Her eyebrows arched in surprise, and if the knock had not come at the door at that moment, Joshua knew she would have said she was from there also. Instead, she raced to fling the plank door open wide. A wiry, rumpled man gave Joshua a cursory glance, then raced to the bedside and knelt by the woman. Out of the corner of his eye, Joshua caught Callie grabbing a bonnet from the peg and tying the strings beneath her chin before she leaned against the wall.

The emotional—the physical and mental stress of traveling across Indian territory and not knowing what he would find— had drained Joshua. He asked himself for the thousandth time

14

if he had done the right thing—coming here, slipping through a break in the mission fence, and listening as Callie stood outside the cabin conversing with this man who now knelt by the pregnant woman. Watching. Waiting. Until he heard the woman inside cry out and knew instinctively he could help.

Mentally, Joshua berated himself. This was no time for questioning his decision. Coming here was the only thing he *could* do. He had planned this for five years, praying fervently all that time that Callie would take one look at him and remember who he was.

☙

Callie could remember how many times she had looked at him—the "stranger," as she had begun to think of him. The muscles of his jaw formed lines tears would follow, if he ever allowed them to fall; but somehow he didn't give the appearance of being soft and sensitive. Yet his powerful body moved gracefully, every movement calculated and smooth. There was a smattering of freckles across the bridge of his nose, apparently caused by being too long in the sun.

Now, he disappeared into the darkness toward David Zeisberger's cabin, where she had insisted he go to properly introduce himself to the elder. Watching him leave, she was possessed by a strange urge to call him back and demand explanations. No, she wouldn't do it. She was not going to give him the satisfaction of knowing she was curious. So she had no answers.

Callie glanced over to the table where Suzannah's husband, Abe, sat. He had been in his work clothes since early this morning, and his clay-brown hair carried creases where he had run his fingers through it the last time. When she had admitted Abe to the cabin, he barely noticed the outsider as he crossed the room, sat beside his wife, and began to pray over and over, "Please, God, not again."

The same petition had echoed deep in Callie's soul as well.

She had been called to the cabin that morning, fearing the worst and hoping she was wrong. The worst didn't happen, but not due to anything she had done. She shook her head to rid herself of her dark thoughts, then cleared her throat. The sound apparently startled Abe, for he stretched and looked across the room at her.

"How can you be sure she will be all right?" He gazed at his wife. Asleep, Suzannah looked like a delicate flower that might fall apart in a strong wind. Cinnamon hair lay in soft curls around her neck, contrasting with her pale face.

How could she explain what she didn't know herself? But Abe was not asking about the babies, and that allowed her to speak with a confidence she didn't feel. "I am sure," she stated, averting her eyes.

Abe sighed. "Where did that fellow come from, anyway? He did not come through the mission entrance."

"No?" She had guessed Abe had directed the stranger to the Solomon home. Uneasily, Callie began to wonder about the wisdom of her decision not to challenge the man.

Abe rubbed his hands together. "No. Pretty sure about that. I was sitting out there—keeping myself occupied, you know?"

Callie knew very well what Abe meant. The last time they had been through this, Abe had sat on the same tree stump. That memory reminded her she needed to tell Abe about the twins Suzannah now carried, but Callie kept thinking of two patches of brown dirt and the words the stranger had murmured, "One of them. . ."

Callie wiped at her eyes, unable to find a way to say something that would cause Abe more grief than any man deserved to bear.

"You do not have to stay if you are tired," Abe admonished. He pushed away from the table before bending over and hanging his hands between his knees. "I can come get you if she gets worse."

"I will be fine." Callie looked at Suzannah, who lay with a hand across her brow. "Besides, you need rest, too. Brother David said he would put you up for the night. Why do you not go on over there?"

Brother David Zeisberger had the largest cabin in the mission. A two-story building, it had been built with extra rooms upstairs for the many friends who came from time to time. Inviting one of their own to spend the night was one way of taking care of the flock.

Abe raised his head. "I would rather be here."

Callie couldn't blame him. When he left earlier, his whole world had been falling apart. *I am sure he can scarcely believe Suzannah is not losing the baby,* Callie thought. She corrected herself: twins.

"He never said who he was, did he?" Abe looked at her intently.

"No, he did not," Callie confessed, wondering if that sounded as strange to Abe as it did to her. Why hadn't she asked his name? On top of that, why had she allowed a stranger to treat Suzannah, of all people? What had she been thinking? To hide her frustration, Callie moved to check on Suzannah. As she positioned herself to listen for Suzannah's breathing, a lingering bitter odor from the medicine used earlier rose up to greet her. The smell made no sense, but there was no time to explore why.

Abe paced the floor for a while, then turned to face her. "What did he do?"

There was a hint of disbelief in his voice, and it caused Callie to pause momentarily. She checked Suzannah's pulse. Slow and steady, unlike her own. *How do I know it was him? How do I know what I had already done did not have something to do with it?* But she knew Abe was aware of what had happened the last time Suzannah had been entrusted to Callie's care. The memory caught in the back of her throat.

"He called it a family secret," she finally admitted.

"I am glad she is safe. . .but, a family secret, Callie? And you do not know what he used?"

Callie straightened Suzannah's bedding and ran a hand across her forehead. "Suzannah is fine now." She returned to sit at the table and noticed the candle was almost burned out. She lit another, and the haze of beeswax filled the air as the flame danced and caught.

Across the room, Suzannah stirred, then pushed up on one arm. "Callie?" she called in a trembling voice.

Callie raced to the woman's side, with Abe close on her heels. "What is it?" She dreaded what she might hear.

"Pain. Again." Suzannah bit her lip, and Callie saw her own tears reflected back in Suzannah's amber eyes.

It was unkind, but Callie's first thought was that the stranger had not solved the problem after all.

ᢞ

Joshua knocked at the door that had been pointed out to him when he left the Solomon home. It was early morning now, his favorite time of day. Soon the nighttime owls' calls would be replaced by the sound of rain crows, and sleepy dawn would begin to illuminate the trees.

Through the yellowed paper covering a window, the blurry silhouette of a man could be seen. Joshua knew he had found the man he sought. It had been five years since he'd had any contact with anyone in the settlement, and he was not sure how his appearance would be received.

David Zeisberger opened the door carrying a handmade candle that cast eerie shadows on the wooden frame and drew attention to the smudges under his somber gray eyes.

"Joshua! Is it really you?" David studied him as if he did not believe what he saw. "Of course it is," he continued. "No other man would dare travel so far alone! And who else would arrive at this hour?"

Joshua smiled. "I am glad you remember me, Brother David."

"You are a man not likely to be forgotten," David replied. "Except by her. . ." he added quietly as he drew Joshua into the cabin.

Joshua looked around, absorbing the room David called home. It was small but neatly kept. A spindly legged table sat in the middle, surrounded by four chairs made in the same rough style. A wooden bowl filled with porridge was surrounded by eating utensils, and the aroma of baked bread hung in the air. A hand-woven throw rug lay under a sturdy shelf Joshua identified immediately as the elder's work space. A scattering of papers covered the top—notes and sermons David planned to speak from in the future.

"It is good to see you!" David's words were heavy with German heritage. "But you did not come here to visit with me, did you?" He filled mugs and offered one to Joshua.

Joshua took a seat at the plank table where David motioned. "You are right, of course. I guess you could say memories could not keep me away any longer," Joshua responded, feeling the familiar twinge of regret that always accompanied the word.

"I see." David settled into his chair and sipped at his coffee. Steam wafted up, disappearing just before it reached his chin.

"My family lost everything. We couldn't keep them. I thank God daily that you happened to be in Philadelphia during the flood. If you had not been, who knows what would have happened to them. . . ." Joshua drew a deep breath as regret once again pressed against his heart.

Am I doing the right thing? The thought slipped into his mind, forcing him to contemplate what had already happened. He had expected her to dispute his right to walk into the home and tend to the woman. After all, her quizzical expression had revealed that she had no idea who he was, and several times she had looked as if she thought to do just that. Each time she had said nothing, letting her silent gaze speak for itself.

David's eyes flashed with curiosity, and his comment was more statement than question. "You have come to stay, then."

Joshua drained the cup, which had cooled while he and David spoke. "If you do not think my presence here will be disruptive, that is my hope."

"We would have to find something for you to do."

"Do not forget that after the disaster I spent some time in medical school." Joshua closed his eyes, remembering. "I did not quite finish the entire course, but I will help any way I can. If there is nothing here for me, I will. . ."

His words faded into nothing. To find, after traveling so far, that Calliope did not remember him would be the end of all he hoped for. In his youth he had been impatient. He did not seem to have learned much patience since then.

Embers snapped in the fireplace behind him and Joshua glanced into the flames. Would the dream he had nurtured for years die when she discovered who he was? No, life would be a bitter battle if that were so. He had trusted in God to keep her safe and God had answered that prayer. Joshua had found her. But how could he tell her he had come to keep the promise she had given shortly before the flood? His good intentions had been swept away when he'd entered the cabin a few hours earlier and she'd had no obvious reaction to him.

"Finding work is not the problem," David said, interrupting Joshua's reverie. Joshua glanced to the slight-statured man who always seemed to have the time and capacity to answer any question he had ever asked. "I do not brag when I say leading a group of Indian followers is not an easy thing to do. We were fortunate to leave Pennsylvania and the pressure of white settlements, where people suspected I was forming some sort of Indian revolt."

"How many accompanied you here?" Joshua asked.

"Five families last spring. A hundred more people joined us last fall, taxing our meager stores throughout the winter." David waved a hand in the air. "But that is not the point of our discussion. We were talking about finding work for you, were we not?"

Joshua nodded.

"We are not exempt from illness. But it would mean—"

"I would have contact with Calliope," Joshua interjected. "Is that what you are afraid of?"

The corners of David's eyes flared. "Calliope? I had forgotten that was her name before. . ." David straightened his shoulders and folded his arms in front of his chest. "How did you find her? We left no trail that I know of."

Joshua noticed David had not asked how he had found *them*. Just her.

"Martin Mack." Joshua had run into Martin when the missionary made a fortuitous trip to Philadelphia. David and Martin had worked for years converting Delaware Indians, and anyone else they could, to Christ before David had led his group away from developing hostilities.

"Did he know what you really were looking for?" David asked pointedly.

Joshua was hurt that David would think he had hidden the truth. "Do you think I would lie to him?"

"Forgive me. I did not mean to imply you had." David gave Joshua a half-smile. "It is just. . .having you suddenly show up. . .I am not sure what it will do to her."

"She has already seen me." Joshua shifted against the wooden slats of the chair, which suddenly seemed hard and uncomfortable. "And she did not remember who I was. Does that make it any easier?"

❧

Callie sipped the remains of a cup of tea she had brewed. She propped her elbows on the table and watched as the dull light outside the window began to brighten. Bread crumbs lay on the tabletop, and she swept them into a pile. Suzannah was asleep again. Abe paced back and forth; his worried steps making soft crunching sounds on the straw-covered dirt floor.

Hours ago it had all seemed so hopeless, Suzannah panting and crying in pain, twisting her arms around her distended abdomen as if she could arrest the delivery. Now, Suzannah's face was calm; and though her springy curls lay limp against her forehead, she showed no signs of discomfort. Whatever the stranger had given Suzannah had worked. But for how long? Callie wondered. And what would happen if he left and she had none of the medicine he had used?

She couldn't let him go without bargaining for some of his potions, Callie decided. She would do whatever it took to present her friend with two beautiful living infants to replace the ones Suzannah had lost.

"Since she is resting, I am going home, then to service," Callie said softly. "I will return after that." She glanced at Suzannah one more time to assure herself the crisis was over.

Abe's eyes followed hers. "All right."

Strolling down the path, Callie recalled how the stranger had marched into the cabin as if he had a right to be there. His attitude had been one of forbearance, as if he understood her despair.

The sounds of awakening children carried through the walls of the log cabins sprinkled about the hilltop where the mission stood, and she pictured the children rising and racing outside to play before eating. Interspersed among the sturdy cabins were simpler, temporary structures built of saplings and bark laced together. Callie and Sarah were fortunate to have one of the finished homes that had ended up being too small for families, and it was toward this structure that she was heading.

"Morning." A deep rumble jolted her from her thoughts.

"Good morning," she replied automatically, though the

resonance of his voice sent her pulse racing. She put a hand up to shield her eyes from the early morning sunlight. He hadn't gone! Hope rose within her as she realized she still had the opportunity to ask him to leave some of the medicine that had helped Suzannah behind when he left.

"The woman?" His voice had turned flat, with no trace of the compassion he had shown last night.

"Sleeping. And her name is Suzannah." Callie didn't know why, but she wanted him to call the woman by her name.

"No problems?"

Callie thought back to what she had done shortly after he left. "Not really," she hedged.

He inhaled sharply. "She needed another dose then?"

Callie paused, then answered. "Yes. She did."

He rested his hands on his hips while he looked at some distant point. "Powerful medicine should be used sparingly."

Callie paled. If she had done anything she shouldn't have, she would never forgive herself. "Did I hurt her?"

"I would not have left it if it could cause harm." He reached out to touch her arm in what she assumed was a gesture of friendship. Friendship or no, his touch was warm, and tingles surged through her. She struggled to look calmly up into those magnificent blue eyes.

"I did not get a chance to ask last night. . ." she began. "Who are you?"

He left his hand on her arm while his gaze swept the length of her plain dress, stopped at her wrinkled apron, then traveled on to the worn moccasins on her feet.

I should be insulted by his scrutiny, Callie thought distractedly. But she wasn't. She had the eerie feeling she knew him, but that was impossible, wasn't it? If she had met him during the last five years, she would have remembered. A shadow covered her heart. *What about the years before that?*

He was staring at her shoes and Callie remembered the

moccasins she had thrown on in haste yesterday morning. He pointed to them. "Your shoes?"

"I made them." She wondered why he was so interested in her footwear. The moccasins were soft and supple and worn by nearly everyone at the mission. "It is just something I learned from the Delawares," she said, as if it did not take weeks of hard work to make a pair just the right size.

He lowered the saddlebag from his shoulder to the ground, and she watched as his eyes roamed over the settlement. A small smile flitted with his mouth as he watched some children tossing sticks into a pile near the clearing.

"Did you introduce yourself to Brother David?" she asked. If he had, she would run over there and find out. She could not call him Magicworker to his face.

"Aye-ya."

No, she told herself, she was twenty-three. She would not run to Brother David. "Who did you tell him you were, then?"

Morning sun highlighted a patch of gleaming black hair and brought out his ruddy complexion. "Joshua."

She stared. "That is it? Just Joshua?"

"Just Joshua." A grin crinkled his lips.

"I suppose the rest is a family secret, too?"

"Could be," he drawled.

He was enjoying dragging this on, she realized. She wasn't. This family secret business was becoming frustrating. But she did like talking with him, liked the way he cut his sentences short as if there were better things in life to move on to.

Move on! There was that thought again that he might leave. Why did it dismay her so? *It is because of what he knows about medicine,* she told herself.

He chuckled suddenly. "No. There is more. It is Johnston."

"What?" She was so convinced he was leaving that the name had thrown her off balance.

"Last name is Johnston."

"Oh. Your name. I thought you meant that is where you are going." Callie posed a finger under her chin. "Joshua Johnston." She liked the way the words rolled off her tongue. She reminded herself that she should be on her way home to wash up and change then off to church, before returning to Suzannah.

"Going to check on Suzannah," Joshua said, withdrawing his hand from her arm. The spot he had been touching grew cold.

Callie stepped back. "Me? No. I am on my way home."

They stood quietly for a moment, and under his scrutiny she lost track of her thoughts.

"No. Me. That is where *I* am going," he said.

Callie could not resist smiling a little. It seemed to amuse him.

"Good thoughts?"

"Only that I hope Suzannah will be all right," she assured him.

"She will." Joshua said it so softly she had to lean forward to hear him.

"I hope so."

"Your name?" He held a finger in front of his lips.

A look of confusion drew her brows together.

"Going to work with you, so might as well know your name," he quipped in a way that said he did not care if he learned it or not.

She crossed her arms in front of her. Should she tell him? She knew his name, and a fine one it was.

"Callie Troyer. And what do you mean work with me?"

He was leaving, wasn't he? That's what men of his sort did. They floated in and drifted out, leaving only a memory and gradual healing behind. Why did the thought of him going seem so depressing?

"Your elder asked me to stay."

Callie swallowed hard. Brother David, staunch Christian and Moravian missionary, had asked him to stay? What did Brother David know that she didn't? Did he expect an epidemic? Or worse, did he not trust her to care for the settlers anymore?

There is an advantage, she told herself. If he stays, then she would have access to his medicine, and that would help Suzannah and anyone else who might come down with an illness she couldn't handle.

She frowned, motioned down the path. "You know where the Solomon cabin is. Her husband is with her," she snapped.

"Where a man should be when his wife is in danger," Joshua said.

"You do not think that is strange?" Most men had little to do with their wives when illness or childbirth happened.

"Absolutely not."

"You should be going, then. To check on Suzannah, I mean." She stepped back to indicate she was finished.

"On my way." He picked up the saddlebag and slung it over his shoulder. "And Callie?"

"Yes?" she replied, telling herself she should not look so eager.

"Have you not remembered me yet?"

three

Callie squinted into the sun to explore his face. "Remember you? I surely do not think so." Yet, inside her ran a tremor of hope. If he knew her. . .

His brows narrowed, drawing the small lines around his eyes tighter. His jaw was covered by a light dusting of beard that she hadn't noticed last night. Beneath the work shirt he wore, his shoulders looked a yard wide.

Not sure what to say, she added, "I do not recall ever meeting you." She spoke evenly, hiding the thread of excitement that ran through her. She would definitely have remembered him if she had ever met him.

"I thought not." Joshua shifted the bag on his shoulder.

"But I should?"

He nodded, a brief dip of his head that caused a tuft of hair to escape from beneath the brim of his hat. He took off the hat and tossed his head to return the lock to its rightful place. The movement was simple, yet sunlight caught and danced in his eyes.

"From where?"

"Pennsylvania."

A giant hand squeezed her chest. "I did live there—once. Before. . .well, before I joined up with the Moravians."

He stared at her as if he expected her to continue. She didn't.

"So did I," he admitted, settling the slouch hat on the back of his head at a jaunty angle that she thought framed his face nicely.

"I think perhaps you have confused me with someone else." She laughed. It felt so easy to talk with him. And he was a traveler, someone who would leave soon. Surely she could risk a few minutes of joy with someone she would not see ever again once he was gone.

Joshua's eyes held her prisoner. "No. I have the right person. You lived in an orphanage, right?"

"Yes," she muttered. "But that was five years ago. Since then I have traveled and lived with Brother David and his flock."

Joshua crossed his arms in front of him. "I know when you joined them."

There was pain in his words and she wondered why something like that would cause him so much hurt. She looked nervously around the mission. "You knew Brother David then, before this morning?"

He nodded. "I helped after the flood."

"The flood." Callie sighed and shook her head. "I do not recall much about that part of my life—only what my sister Sarah remembers. Since she is younger than I, she is not much help." She didn't remember anything from before that, either, but Joshua didn't need to know that.

"I figured as much." He stepped toward her.

Tendrils of worry stirred in the pit of her stomach. She turned to a safer topic. "I have heard the west end of Philadelphia was swept away."

He set his lips in a grim line. "It was terrible. No warning. Heavy rains. People were lost. We saved those we could."

A shadow veiled his consistently warm eyes. Something had hurt him in the flood—Callie sensed it instinctively. Not wanting to drag up memories she didn't possess but he obviously did, she offered, "It must have been quite a shock."

"You could say that." He turned away, leaving her feeling as if she had touched on a sensitive area that she should have stayed away from.

"If there is nothing else, I must go." She started walking toward her home, then turned around abruptly. "Oh! I have not said a proper thank-you for what you did for Suzannah last night."

"That is not necessary. It is what I have been trained to do." His words were strained. Why did everything she said make him uneasy?

"Callie!" Sarah rushed toward them, her strawberry-blond braid flopping up and down as she ran. A smile curved Callie's lips in welcome as she momentarily forgot about Joshua.

Sarah was sixteen—gangly, awkward, and likely to say whatever crossed her mind. But knowing she could have lost Sarah made Callie love her that much more. As Sarah came to a stop, Callie reached out and patted her cheek.

"I want you to meet someone who once lived in Pennsylvania, Sarah," she began, turning to introduce her sister to Joshua.

But he was gone, half the settlement away, and knocking on the Solomon cabin door. Callie felt as if she were watching the scene from far off and gave Sarah a weak half-smile. "Guess he was in a hurry," she said. "You will have to meet him later."

Sarah gazed at the handsome figure he cut, his head coming almost to the top of the door frame. "I will make it a point to. He looks mighty good from this distance."

Callie held up a hand, but Sarah rushed on. "Do not bother to chastise me for thinking that. By the light in your eyes, your thoughts are exactly the same."

"Why, I never!" Callie exclaimed, though a red tinge of a blush filled her cheeks.

"Have you been at the Solomons' all night?" Sarah asked, changing the subject. "Is Suzannah all right? Is there a baby?"

Callie straightened Sarah's braid. "One at a time," she said gently. "I was just on my way home to tell you. She will be fine. No baby yet. Which is a good thing, I might add."

"No baby? What did you use? Last time you said you did

not have anything to make her pains stop."

Callie's stomach curled into a tight knot. "Actually, he gave her something to make her sleep." She rubbed her arms, which suddenly felt as if she had been swimming in an icy river.

Sarah kicked at a pebble and her head bobbed as she watched the stone hop across the grass. "Levi came looking for you a few minutes ago."

Callie stiffened, the knot in her stomach growing even larger. "I thought the hunters were not due back for another week?"

Sarah shrugged. "Got back early." She grinned. "Says he has something important to ask you."

Two days' worth of tiredness washed over Callie. "No rumors, Sarah. I am not marrying him."

Sarah smiled dreamily. "He thinks you are. And is it not about time you settled down?"

Yes, it probably was about time she settled down. Most women her age had been married for five or six years, but Callie could not see spending the rest of her life with Levi. There was nothing specifically wrong with him. He was Suzannah's brother and could out-hunt any of the Delawares in their mission. However, hunting was not high on her list of requirements for a mate.

Her thoughts stopped as quickly as they had begun. She had no right to categorize what she wanted in a husband. God put man here first, then added woman to walk with him. She should be thankful Levi seemed to care about her, especially since others in her life had found her relatively easy to cast off.

"How about breakfast?" she queried to change the subject.

"Already ate," Sarah said. "You going to church?"

"As soon as I clean up."

"I told Levi he would probably find you there." Sarah giggled as she hurried away.

Callie clasped her hands in front of her and stared at them.

Levi Lyons was back. He had something important to ask her. She knew what that would be. Why did the thought scare her so?

Marriage was a blending of souls, a merging of dreams. It was having someone beside you through good and bad. Someone who cared about you, someone who believed in God, and you, and made you more than you ever thought you could be by yourself. The problem with Levi Lyons was that he did not do those things for her.

She wanted a love like Suzannah and Abe had. A love that knew no bounds, encouraged hope, and made tomorrow seem like an exciting promise instead of just another day. And there again, Levi did not measure up.

Perhaps there is something wrong with me, Callie mused. Maybe, in the end, it was best she not fall in love. Even though it meant she would be alone, at least she would not have to face carrying a child for nine months only to lose it.

Joshua's rugged profile haunted her and she tried again to remember him. The attempt was fruitless, but she vowed that the next time she saw him, she would demand he tell her more about what he apparently knew. A colt whinnied, and Callie walked across the path and stroked his mane.

"Hey, fellow," she said to the bay whose head reached almost to her shoulder. "You hungry?" The colt tossed his head and Callie chuckled at his seemingly human response.

People were moving about, headed toward the meeting house for the morning service. She forced her feet to carry her home to the sparsely furnished cabin she and Sarah shared. Home to eat, to change clothes, to put on something a little more respectable than this worn-out, dingy gray dress.

❧

The morning service lasted long enough for a few hymns and a short sermon. Most Moravian congregations were separated into "choirs," which consisted of groups of single men, single women, widows, widowers, and married couples. The Delawares refused to be separated from their families in such a manner, so they were allowed to scatter as they wished throughout the building.

Callie arrived at the meeting house as Brother David strode in a back door. Sliding onto a bench in the back, she glanced around the building that was the first permanent structure always built at a Moravian mission.

Love, sweat, and laughter enabled the settlers to assemble the logs that became a thirty-six-by-forty-foot worship center. No windows were included in the design, and candles positioned down the walls every five feet provided soft golden light by which the settlers prayed, worshiped, and had fellowship.

The sleek dark heads of the Delaware Indians, called "Praying Indians" by some, filled the seats ahead of her, their broken English mingling with their native language. Almost a year had passed since she had traveled with Brother David and his flock to establish the settlement they called "Schoenbrunn." The name meant "Hill of Grace," and Callie was not alone in thinking it perfect.

Deep in the wilderness where a bear roamed occasionally and wolves howled at night, Schoenbrunn Mission sat on top of a rolling plain with a roaming river not far away. Grace was abundant here, for the mission thrived on loving Jesus and the freedom to do so.

Callie admired the way the whole village worked to overcome obstacles and concentrate on the positive. No one talked about it, especially the Delawares, but danger lurked. East and north of them, the French and British were hoarding land and running out natives who had lived there for generations. Even though the Moravians had located miles from white pioneers who Brother David said would keep pushing farther west until they ran out of land, it worried Callie that they might not be safe even here.

Several of the children she worked with in Sunday lessons smiled at her, and their broad-faced grins affirmed for her that they were doing the right thing. They didn't seem to mind that she was one of few whites living here. Nor did it matter that they had only known her for five years.

At the front of the room, Brother David raised his arms and bent his head. His coat fell open to reveal a gray vest over a white shirt and knee-high moccasins. "Shall we pray?"

Callie bowed her head while the elder thanked God for His blessings, Jesus for His sacrifice, and the congregation for their belief in God's grace. She added her own plea that Suzannah carry the twins closer to term before giving birth.

"One of them. . ." Joshua's puzzling words echoed in her mind until Brother David's enthusiastic "Amen" pushed it away.

She raised her head and readied her mind to concentrate on the elder's message. When she looked at David, she caught sight of Joshua in the front row. He looked peaceful and rested, which annoyed her. Having spent most of the night with Suzannah as she had, she had expected him to look tired. And hadn't he been traveling yesterday? She knew he must have been, yet he didn't look worn out at all.

Levi Lyons slid into the seat beside her, and her thoughts retreated. Levi liked to do things that were shocking to most, and today was no exception. He gave her a broad smile as he stretched out a hand to squeeze one of hers briefly. Remembering how Joshua had covered her hand before he prayed last night, she compared Levi's hand to Joshua's. Levi's hands could aim at a deer with surety or skin a beaver with confidence, but when he moved his hand away and let it drop across his thigh, Callie was relieved.

"Sorry I am late," he whispered. "I overslept." His curly red hair fell in disarray over his ears and his eyes were blurry with sleep.

"I am glad you are back," she acknowledged and turned to the front of the room.

Levi leaned toward her to say something, but Callie discreetly pointed to Brother David, who was just beginning to speak about the need for forgiveness. Levi seemed uneasy. He shifted and squirmed in his seat until the elder was finished. Callie didn't think it was because he was uncomfortable with the elder's message. More likely, he was getting up the courage to ask her that "important question."

The last words of praise faded into the rafters and a rare smile played on Brother David's face as he approached the stranger sitting in the front row.

"I would like everyone to meet the newest member of our settlement," he began.

Joshua stretched to his full height and faced the congregation. Every move he made seemed calculated to get the most from his energy. With his buckskin coat slung over one shoulder and that slouch hat dangling from one hand, Joshua commanded respect. The blurry image of a memory tugged at Callie but shifted just out of focus. She twisted her hands together.

"This is Joshua Johnston," Brother David said excitedly. "He will be staying, and I have invited him to use his medical training to assist Callie." David's gaze moved through the crowd until he found Callie. "We know what a difficult time she has keeping one hundred sixty people well," he added.

Several heads bobbed in agreement, but darkness engulfed Callie. She felt the beginnings of discomfort at Joshua's appearance. He had asked if she remembered him. Did that have something to do with him coming here?

The elder continued, his rich baritone echoing around the room, drawing her away from her thoughts about Joshua's intentions.

"Joshua seeks to aid us in our quest for health and happiness. Some of you will call him a Magicworker, but what he brings to

Schoenbrunn is God's healing. I know you will welcome him," he finished, motioning to Joshua that it was his turn to speak.

Callie had no trouble envisioning Joshua curing sickness; he had already stopped Suzannah's babies from coming too soon. He did not, however, appear to be a man who would settle for simply helping her. She wished she knew more about him.

Joshua addressed the room, and the majority of the settlers pressed forward to welcome him. Levi took advantage of the momentary confusion to escort her outside. He grabbed her arm a little too abruptly for her liking, but she followed since the meeting house hardly seemed the place to make a scene.

"Does Brother David think you do not know what you are doing?" Levi grumbled. "I do not like the way that fellow looks."

"I do not see anything wrong with him. There are times when I do need help."

Her dress stuck to her back, where beads of perspiration had formed, and she glanced longingly toward one of the lush shade trees that lined the mission.

"You have never complained before." Levi's voice rose a notch. "You mark my words. He will be trouble."

"Mr. Johnston will be a fine addition to our mission," Callie stated calmly. "Should we not let him prove himself before we begin belittling him?"

"What do you mean by that?" There definitely was displeasure in Levi's voice now.

When he started courting her, she would let him have his say. But after a time, a pocket of confidence formed deep inside her.

"He stopped your sister's labor last night," she informed him, successfully hiding her irritation that the stranger had been able to do so when she had not.

Levi's eyes widened.

"You did not know, did you?"

"No," he growled. "I got back late. After. . .not going to lose. . ." He turned away.

Hiding tears? Callie didn't think so. Nothing appeared to touch Levi's heart. He had dug the graves for his angelic nieces nine months ago without emotion, while she watched, unable to hold in her own sorrow.

"Suzannah is fine now." She regretted not stopping to think that he might not yet have heard.

Levi mumbled something, then sped in the direction of his sister's home.

Callie sighed. She spotted her sister ahead of her on the path, and she hurried to catch up with her. Callie reminded Sarah that she needed to finish the leggings she had been working on. She assured Callie that she would head home right away to do so. Hearing that, Callie turned her steps toward the Solomons' cabin, hoping Levi had already left there.

With morning in full bloom, the sun kissed the treetops and the roosters had fallen silent. In the clearing where future log homes would be built, men who had hurried from the service spoke animatedly with one another.

Callie loved being outside, where blue jays darted back and forth, the rush of the river could be heard in the near distance, and where the world seemed as right as in the Garden of Eden. She undid the ties that held her bonnet under her chin. After removing it, she let the long, thin ties trail on the ground as she walked the remainder of the way to Suzannah's.

⁊⁊

Joshua sipped from his cup, swirling the remains at the bottom. After checking on Suzannah and shaking hands with those in the meeting house who welcomed him, he had returned to the elder's for the morning meal.

Though he had been in the home earlier, he had missed noticing the front of the house actually had two small rooms:

one for eating and one for sleeping. An archway opened onto a back room, where a door led outside to a covered walkway connected to the meeting house.

Joshua glanced at the man who was like a father to him. He wanted—no, he needed—the elder's support as Joshua attempted to free himself from the demons that had chased him for what seemed like decades. Their previous conversation had only given him a place to stay and a job to do.

"You do not think I have made a wise decision by coming here, do you?" Joshua tried to keep his voice respectful.

David opened his arms in a questioning gesture. "I think I know what you are trying to do," he began. "And I will admit that I am uncomfortable with it."

Joshua struggled past the knot forming in his throat. "I asked Calliope this morning if she had remembered me yet. Do you know what she did?"

Despite the loyalty he had for the man who had shown him Jesus, Joshua's gaze sought the security of his coffee mug. For a moment he glimpsed the Calliope he remembered lying on the ground, a piece of a quilt tucked under her chin and blond curls plastered against a deathly pale face.

The dark liquid in the cup reminded him of her eyes so long ago—empty, blank, containing nothing of what the two of them had shared. *Just like last night in the Solomon home,* he thought. *She does not recognize me.* The realization scared him. His mouth grew dry. What if she never did?

"She is Callie now," David gently reminded. "What did she say?" He leaned forward, his brow pulling his gray eyes tighter together.

Joshua pushed away the last image he carried of a younger Calliope. David was right. She was Callie. She had survived. That should be enough, but it wasn't.

"She looked at me without any emotion on her face whatsoever." Joshua swallowed hard, his Adam's apple rising then falling. "How could she not remember?"

A silent, masculine tear brushed the edge of his eye. He ignored it.

David pushed an unruly tuft of hair behind one ear. "How long do you think it will be before you tell her the truth?"

"I do not plan to come right out and tell her," Joshua insisted. "I came to see if she had survived."

So many times he had thought about that night. The screaming, the crashing, the loss. He was committed now. Until he put it behind him, one way or another, there would be no sense of closure, no loosening of the bonds that tied him to this woman everyone here called Callie.

David's expression lightened. "I believe you. And if it is of any help, you are not in this alone. But how long do you plan to stay? When will enough time have elapsed?"

He knew David had spent years planning, shaping, and forging new dreams, but time meant nothing to him anymore.

"When she remembers me, then I will deal with the rest." Did the words have to drag his heart out with them?

David leaned back, slowly shaking his head from side to side. "She will not be easy to convince."

Joshua's voice thickened. "I know." He felt drained, his entire being saturated with exhaustion. "But I will do it. It is the only thing I can give her that means anything anymore."

David's fingers tapped reverently on his Bible. "It is a good thing you are a praying man, for you will need to walk with God now as never before."

"You once told me faith made all things possible, David. Does it not apply to this situation also?" Joshua covered his brow with one hand.

"Hebrews eleven," David said. "Faith is the substance of things hoped for, the evidence of things not seen." He stopped talking for a minute. "Faith makes things possible, Joshua. It does not make them easy."

Joshua snapped his head up. "If love was easy, it would not be worth having."

four

Sarah looked across the room as Callie entered the cabin and deposited some logs by the door. While the days warmed quickly, the nights held a chill that could only be chased away by a fire.

"Well? What did you find out?"

"He is from Pennsylvania," Callie muttered as she dropped onto the edge of a chair. She had just come from a meeting with Brother David and Joshua. "In fact, he lived at the same orphanage we did."

Why did it sound so unbelievable, even though she'd repeated it at least a hundred times to herself?

"The same orphanage!" Sarah slipped into a seat across from her sister, settling the folds of her long skirt neatly on her lap. "That is exciting, Callie!"

Callie struggled to remain calm while recalling the visit. She had been summoned to Brother David's and had gone thinking he wanted to discuss the illnesses sweeping through the mission. Joshua had been waiting when she arrived.

Despite every bit of common sense that told her she should pay no attention to him, Callie thought Joshua looked quite noble. The fire drew out auburn highlights in the thick dark locks that hung splendidly over his ears. He sat casually in a chair, his legs stretched out to their tremendous length in front of him.

As she listened to Brother David tell her he expected her to give Joshua her full support, Callie remembered Levi's reaction when he returned from the hunt and found Joshua would be working alongside her. Levi had certainly been displeased but wouldn't explain why. Sometimes she didn't understand Levi, more so lately than ever before. Why had he warned her to stay away from Joshua?

Callie sighed. The way things were, she would never know. Levi would think it disgusting if she challenged him to explain.

"I would not call it exciting, Sarah. I would call it. . ." What would she call it? Confusing? Worrisome? Why had Brother David asked Joshua to assist her? It was quickly becoming a muddle, and she saw no way to solve it.

"I cannot wait to tell MaryBeth!" Sarah pulled a bonnet out of an apron pocket and smoothed it into place over her curls.

"No, Sarah." Callie's voice turned brittle. "This is not something you are to talk about." Why was she warning her sister? What was there about Joshua that made her so skittish?

"But I have got to share this with her," Sarah whined. "I would think you would be delighted that someone has shown up who knew you before the flood. I have never been much help, since they kept me on a separate floor, but this," Sarah clapped her hands excitedly, "is what you have always wanted. Is it not?"

"I used to think so." Callie drew a deep breath. "Now I am not so sure. That is why I do not want you to speak of it to anyone just yet." She looked pleadingly into her sister's eyes, whose color reminded her of tanned buckskin. "Do as I ask. Please?"

A look of disappointment flitted across Sarah's round face. "I will not tell MaryBeth. Or anyone else."

Callie eyed Sarah closely. "Promise?"

Sarah nodded, her long braid bobbing as she did. "God's promise. That is better than just a plain promise."

So it was, Callie thought. People might fail, but God's covenants stood fast. At least *that* she could depend on.

"I have one question, though." Sarah's voice dropped to a whisper.

"What?"

"Do you remember him at all? This Mr. Johnston, I mean."

Callie shook her head, trying to dispel the image of Joshua in Suzannah's cabin that had just erupted there.

"I am not sure I want to. It is all rather confusing just now."

Sarah looked away. "It will all work out for the best. Isn't that what you always tell me?"

"Yes," Callie agreed. "I just wish I knew his real reason for coming here."

Why was she questioning his motives? Since arriving, he had taken part in both morning and evening services. Brother David had announced this morning that Joshua would preach the Sunday sermon. He was her brother-in-Christ, but something about him stirred uneasy feelings deep inside.

"Why do you not simply ask him?"

Sarah's question intruded in her thoughts. "That would hardly be proper. Do you not remember a woman's place in the world? We are to be seen, not heard. Whatever his reason, he will choose when he can reveal it. It is not my place to pry." She threw Sarah a warning glance. "Nor is it yours."

Sarah raised her hands, palms out. "I am going to see MaryBeth. I will not talk about *him*. Do not worry about lunch. I will eat with her."

"Fine," Callie replied. She would use the time to rearrange the herbs and roots in her bag before she went to sit with Suzannah.

With Sarah gone, Callie laid out her meager herb collection. Fragrant aromas drifted up as she arranged and checked the contents of each of the small deerskin pouches. Concentrating on the array of cures Helping Hands had insisted Callie memorize before the Delaware woman left the mission, she didn't hear the knock at the door. As the door swung open, it scraped against the frame, and Callie snapped her head toward it.

It was Levi. His work shirt was stained, his normally curly

red hair thick with sweat and bits of tree bark. He bluntly canvassed the inside of the cabin, which took about four seconds since it was only two small rooms.

"Are you going to ask me in?"

Callie brushed her hands together to remove traces of the herbs. "You can see Sarah is gone. It is more proper that we sit under the tree."

In the time it took to walk outside, she took stock of him. No one could say Levi Lyons didn't do his share to help Schoenbrunn survive. Not only did he help clear land, he went along on hunts for game that would provide them with food and furs. Since the last hunt, something had changed him. Levi no longer seemed the courteous man he had been before.

He motioned toward a gnarled root that grew aboveground. Callie lowered slowly into place and smoothed out her skirt. Levi squatted next to her, rubbing his neck.

"Has your workload lightened since the healer came to stay?" He sounded perturbed.

"He has only been here a few days. That is hardly enough to make a large difference." She brushed at a faint sheen of perspiration that dotted her forehead.

"You need to relax, Callie. Take some time and go on a picnic with me." Levi leaned over and trailed his fingers lightly along her forearm.

His touch was familiar, and it was widely accepted that they would be wed. But Callie had never been comfortable with outward displays of affection and shifted out of his reach.

"I do not know," she argued. "There is so much to do and it never seems to end. I should stay close in case something happens to Suzannah again."

What would she do if her friend, Levi's sister, threatened to miscarry again?

Levi sneered. "I am sure the mysterious Joshua can handle any crisis that crops up."

He leaned toward her. He had been burning brush, and the acrid smell of wood smoke clung to his shirt. She wrinkled her nose.

"I am sure he could," she answered hastily. "But that does not mean I can forget my responsibilities."

Levi's glare sent a chill up her backbone. "Do not do it, Callie," he said sharply. "Do not push me away. We have always been able to talk before. Why have you changed?"

Callie had no choice but to look at him. His green eyes seemed to bore into hers. "I am not the one who has changed and I am not avoiding you, Levi," she insisted. "Running back and forth between houses takes a lot out of me."

Levi pressed his lips together. At the base of his neck, his pulse jumped. "I do not like it. I want to see you, spend time with you."

"That is almost impossible as long as there are people who get sick. You know that."

Levi's shadow shielded her from the sun peeking through a tangle of tree branches. He said *she* had changed. Didn't he realize it was he who was acting so strangely?

"Then we will have to find a way to make it possible, will we not?" His tone matched the tight set to his jaw.

Callie curled her fingers around the root by her side. "I will try to make some time tomorrow," she bargained. "Perhaps Sarah can sit with the Killbuck boy."

"His mother can do it. Is that not what mothers are for?" He walked a few steps away, his hands balled into tight fists at his sides.

Callie was annoyed at the way he suddenly thought she should drop everything and rush away with him.

"Besides the fact that she has been up with him almost constantly, helping out around here is my duty." She paused. She had known Levi ever since she came to live with the Moravians, and he had never acted like this. What was bothering him?

She kept her gaze locked with his. "What happened on your last hunt, Levi?"

Levi drew back. The sun sculpted the tight muscles of his neck and illuminated the shallow circles around his eyes. "What happens on a hunt is not a woman's concern." He glanced toward the clearing, where a man was shouting and waving at him. "There will be a picnic, Callie. Just you and me."

The danger she heard in his tone shocked her. But Levi was stamping away, long, angry steps putting a distance between them that she did not understand or want to explore at that moment.

₰

Behind the meeting house a tangle of brambles began where a small clearing ended. Squirrels and other chattering animals frolicked among the branches overhead. Brother David and Joshua sat on an old piece of buckskin that had been laid out in the late April sun.

David stretched his legs out in front of him. His coat was open, revealing a brown vest over a white shirt. "You were surprised by Callie's question this morning, were you not?"

"Stunned is more like it," Joshua confided. "It is so painful to look at her and remember. . ." He swallowed the rest of his comment. David knew the depth of his pain. There was no need to elaborate.

"Not only God works in mysterious ways." David twirled a blade of grass around his finger. "Sometimes the mind does also."

The brim of Joshua's slouch hat slipped toward his eyebrows. He pushed it back. "Are you saying she may never remember everything about us? That cannot be true! Why would God do that to me?"

"God has His reasons, Joshua. I do not have to remind you of that. It has been hard on her not remembering her life before the flood."

"And you think it was easy for me to let her go? To not know what was happening to her for five years!"

David placed a hand on Joshua's arm. "If you want what is best for her, you may have to do more than face that fact. You may have to let her go."

Joshua watched a hawk sail overhead. He had never thought about the possibility his Calliope might be lost to him forever. "I will not leave here until it is clear there is no hope she will ever remember what we had."

Bittersweet words, but he would never hold a woman to a promise she could not recall. Fear wrapped a hand around his heart. Why had he left her in the first place? If he had stayed with her and foregone the medical training his father had insisted he receive, this might not be happening now.

He had never been one to stand up to his parents, and he wondered if the relationship he had with them would have been ruined had he done so then.

David rubbed his forehead as if he were searching for the correct words. "Even if it means you live out the rest of your life here?"

"If that is what it takes, then I am willing to wait." Joshua rose. Thinking about how long it might take to win Calliope back frightened him. Surely, he thought, if he were patient and made daily contact with her, she would eventually remember. Wouldn't she?

Patience had never characterized Joshua. Sure he had waited five years to search for Calliope, but most of that time was spent helping his parents and then attending medical school in Philadelphia. How long would it be before he said something to her he would regret?

❧

Callie watched Sarah put a loaf of fresh-baked bread on the table to cool. A pot of thin corn soup bubbled in a kettle over the fireplace. The yeasty smell, mixed with the seasonings in the kettle, started a small rumble in her stomach. With so much happening to Suzannah and those who were ill, she realized she had not eaten much in recent days.

"Did you take a nap?" Sarah asked. She had come home from MaryBeth's to find Callie lying on her bed and had left her sister alone while she prepared the evening meal, for once without being prodded to do so.

"No. Levi came by and we talked for a while." Callie said the words quietly, not mentioning his appearance.

"He wants to marry you! I knew it!" Sarah squeezed her hands together in front of her.

"Do not start planning a wedding," Callie warned. The words stuck in her throat like musty bread.

Sarah absently pushed a clump of straw on the floor with the toe of her shoe. "Why do you not love him?" she asked. "He seems very nice to me."

"Love does not come just because someone is nice." Callie smiled apologetically at her sister. "I am sorry, I should not have barked at you. I just meant that love takes time to grow, to develop into something that will last forever."

She felt strange defining love. As an orphan, love came in the simple servings of soup and sometimes potatoes she had gotten for meals. Being a relatively new Christian, love meant trusting in God's grace and Jesus' sacrifice. But love between two people? She knew next to nothing about that aspect of life, despite Sarah's insistence that Levi was destined to be her mate.

"Can we not talk about Levi right now? There are too many other things on my mind."

Sarah stirred the soup. "How is Storm?" She gave her sister an encouraging smile.

"No better. His mother keeps asking when he will be able to get up and play. What am I supposed to tell her?"

Callie had spoken the question aloud without meaning to.

She had hoped to spare Sarah the devastating news that she didn't think three-year-old Storm would survive the high fever he'd had for a day.

Sarah crossed the room, paying no attention to the wooden ladle she had let fall into the soup. She took Callie's hand in her own and turned it back and forth a few times before patting it.

"You can tell me the truth. You are afraid we are going to lose him, are you not?"

Callie fought the tears forming in her eyes. She was supposed to be the strong one. When had Sarah become so perceptive? She had never paid much attention to what went on around her before.

"Whatever happens is God's will."

Sarah dropped into the chair beside Callie's. "Sometimes I do not understand this God we worship," she said. "He took our parents away and tore our family apart, but you insist He loves us. How can you say that, Callie?"

Callie's shoulders hurt and her legs were tired, but she met her sister's gaze squarely. "Because God is love, Sarah. It is not our place to question why He works the way He does."

"I think He could go a little easier on us sometimes."

"He has His reasons."

Callie didn't understand why she could remember only the past five years of her life, and she didn't know why Joshua had shown up now, but she was determined to trust God to reveal the answers at the right time.

Sarah sniffed the air. "Soup is ready."

Callie chuckled. "It does not smell like you have burned it this time."

Sarah rolled her eyes toward the ceiling. "You will never let me forget that, will you?"

"One thing is sure," Callie said with a straight face. "If you do not improve your skills, your future husband may starve."

After a shared chuckle, they sipped the thin broth that would be much better once the vegetables in the garden began to produce.

five

"Will it help?" Kukara Killbuck, Storm's mother, asked between sobs.

Callie waited breathlessly for Joshua's response. The depth of pain in Kukara's eyes made Callie wish she had summoned him sooner to treat little Storm. The boy's life now hung in the balance because of her pride.

Her heart staggered in her chest. How could she have done this? She thought back over the last four days. Storm's fever had risen steadily, no matter what she tried. When she finally realized her treatment was not helping, she called on Joshua. He had given Storm a potion, and they waited now for signs that the medicine was helping.

"We shall see," Joshua offered. His solemn tones underlined the seriousness of the situation.

Callie looked at him, willing him to understand how sorry she was. He glanced at her, but the familiar spark in his eyes that she had begun to look forward to was missing.

She watched Kukara's hand as the slender woman caressed her son's face. Her face was strained, and worry lines etched deep grooves around the edges of her almond-shaped eyes.

How did women endure it? Giving birth and thinking of the hundreds of things that could go wrong? Knowing the small babe you held in your arms might never grow to adulthood? The thoughts unsettled Callie.

Forcing herself not to concentrate on the depressing situation in her midst, Callie tried to find a substitute. Her eyes flitted around the cabin, searching for something familiar. What she found was Joshua staring at her. She would have given almost anything to know what he was thinking.

His face was carved stone, his jaw clenched and his brows drawn together. Then, as if he couldn't look at her any longer, he turned away and watched Storm's chest rise in deep, rasping breaths.

Joshua had grimaced at his first sight of the ill young boy, and Callie had withdrawn into a corner of the cabin rather than face him. She knew he must be disgusted that she had let the child suffer for so long.

"You must do something," Kukara wailed. "He is my only child!"

The agony in her words jolted Callie. What if Storm didn't make it? Panic stirred in her soul. Why hadn't she acted sooner? Would God call her to task when she stood her judgment day? What would she have to say for herself: "I am so sorry I worried more about what Joshua Johnston thought of me than I did about the boy's illness"? No, she didn't think God would approve of that excuse.

"He is doing all he can," Callie heard herself say, despite feeling that her eternity was now condemned to something other than heaven.

Kukara's glance skittered between Joshua and Callie. "There must be more!" She threw a hand against her lips, and the rest of her wail disappeared into her palm.

"Storm is in God's hands now," Joshua admitted.

Kukara grabbed Joshua's elbow. "You are Healer." Tears ran down her cheeks and formed splotches on her deerskin garment. "Save him."

"Kukara." Joshua shook his head. "It is God who can save Storm, not me." He dipped a rag in water and laid it on the boy's forehead, his fingers pressing lightly against the fevered brow.

Callie moved to stand behind Kukara and placed a comforting hand on her shoulder. This was so difficult. *Please, God,* she prayed silently. *Help me say the right thing.*

"We must trust in God," she began, "and in His will." She had tried to sound compassionate, but the grating sound of her voice hung in the air.

"His will takes too long! I want answers now!" Kukara threw herself across her son's limp body, her cries muffled by the thin blanket covering him.

"God's grace comes when He decrees." Joshua backed away from the bed and stood by the wall, but nothing in his manner indicated scorn or discouragement as he leaned against the logs.

"Nothing we do, except prayer, will change that. I must leave; there are others I must tend to." He settled his hat on his head and picked up the saddlebag he carried everywhere.

Callie swallowed a lump of disbelief. He was leaving! How could he, when Storm might be about to die!

Kukara lurched away from her son and clutched at Joshua's sleeve. "You not leave now. You stay with Storm."

Callie held her breath. What would he do? What would she do without him?

He laid a hand over Kukara's. "I will be back after I check on the others. Would you have them go without treatment?" He looked straight into the night-brown eyes of Kukara. "The medicine is working. Listen."

Callie did. Storm's breathing did seem less labored than it had been earlier. His face was still pasty, though. She knew the worst was not over.

"You stay," Kukara repeated. She slipped away and pulled a small pouch from under a wooden crate. "If you go, I use this." She raised her hand and shook the container. Keeping one eye on Joshua, she withdrew a handful of dirt and moved toward her son, where she slowly raised her hand above the boy's head.

"Do not!" Callie and Joshua spoke together, their eyes

meeting, then breaking away to return to Kukara. Tears streamed down the woman's cheeks, creating tracks on her bronzed skin.

"I must give back to Earth-Mother what Earth-Mother gave to me." Kukara's voice held a strand of courage as ancient as the Indian heritage she came from.

Joshua clenched his jaw. Sprinkling dirt on the boy was Kukara's way of committing his soul back to the earth. She was giving up, something he would not let her do.

"We must allow God to do His work," he began as he moved slowly toward her.

Callie noticed how calm he appeared, and silently gave him high marks for his ability to remain unruffled. She certainly was having a hard time maintaining any semblance of control.

Kukara chewed her bottom lip while her hand edged out to hover over her son's chest.

Joshua's sharp glance at Callie stunned her. Was he pleading silently for her to help? She struggled to keep her emotions in check as she tried to figure out what she could do. She hesitated too long. Joshua moved his gaze back to Kukara.

"Have you been doing this all along?" he asked. David had mentioned to him that upon conversion to Christianity, the Delawares had promised to give up their tribal ceremonies and beliefs. He didn't like it, but he could understand how, when faced with tragedy, some might turn back to the comforting traditions they had dismissed.

Kukara appeared torn between wanting to answer him truthfully and giving him the answer she thought he wanted to hear. Though one hand bravely hovered above her son's chest, the other was wrapped tightly in a band of fringe that traveled the length of her long buckskin dress.

"Callie knew," she murmured.

Oh, my, Callie thought. There would be no avoiding Joshua now. She cringed as Joshua jerked his head around to peer at her.

"Is that true?" he demanded. "You are supposed to encourage these people in their new life. How could you allow something like this?"

Her eyes grew tearful at his criticism. Somehow, she had expected him to remain distanced from anything that happened. The fact he had not was disturbing, but she could not put her finger on the reason why.

"I. . .I did not think. . .it would hurt." She had thought she was encouraging Kukara. Yes, the woman had threatened before to return to her old beliefs, but Callie had never taken her seriously. And what did Joshua know of reaching within himself and finding resources he did not know he had to help others?

"You did not think. . ." Joshua blurted. As quickly as he had allowed his irritation to show, he closed his eyes and rolled his head heavenward. "Pray with me."

Callie was grateful for the interruption. At least it meant his accusing eyes were not piercing her. She dropped her head without checking to see what Kukara had done. Joshua's solemn tones filled the room, slowing Callie's heart rate and forcing her to concentrate on something other than the small boy on the cot.

When the prayer ended, Callie did feel calmer, but she saw Kukara's hand shaking as the dirt drifted out in a tiny stream on Storm's chest. Had the woman not been listening to anything Joshua had just said?

An ominous silence filled the cabin. Joshua reached out and gently guided Kukara's trembling hand toward the pouch he now held. Indecision seemed to filter through her eyes. Then, slowly, her hand turned over and dirt sifted from her palm into the pouch.

Joshua smiled cautiously. "Put it away and promise me you will not use it again."

Callie could see Kukara struggling with his request. His large fingers spanned the woman's shoulders easily, and she watched as he focused solely on Kukara. Some monumental bond of trust appeared to spring between them. Kukara nodded.

Storm whimpered and Callie raced to him, trying to still her own quivering shoulders. She bent over the boy, running her hand across his brow and pushing the tangled mass of thick black hair back off his forehead.

The thump behind her startled her, and she swung her head around to find Kukara collapsed on the floor.

❧

Callie watched Joshua carry Kukara to the other bed across the room. It was strange seeing him take care of people who had been her patients. She waited until he backed away, then moved to do what she could. She dipped a cloth in water and wiped the day-old tears from Kukara's face, keeping a safe distance from Joshua. For some reason, she had to concentrate extra hard on the task at hand.

"She will come around," Joshua said over her shoulder.

She hadn't heard him approach, but she gathered her scattered wits and nodded her acknowledgment. "What about Storm?"

"Trust in God."

His voice echoed in the cabin's utter stillness. Icy fear twisted her heart as she recalled he had said the same thing to Kukara earlier. "Then you do not have the answers to every crisis we have here?"

Since she was not looking directly at him, she felt confident in her ability to question him. One look into his lake-deep eyes and she would have forgotten anything but how he had dashed to her rescue—or rather, Storm's rescue, she reprimanded herself.

"I have answers, Callie. But not to the questions you are asking. Only God has those." His eyes narrowed and he touched a finger to the brim of his hat.

She knew he expected her to pursue the conversation, but she didn't feel up to it. "How long have you believed in God?"

"Five years," he replied.

Five years! She would have been eighteen, newly homeless, being cared for by compassionate Moravians, and just discovering she had no memory of her life before the flood.

"You?" His voice dropped to a soothing level and she understood why so many villagers were enamored of him. He was easy to talk to and seemed genuinely eager to listen.

"About the same," she mumbled. Not too long after Callie was taken in by the Moravians, Brother David and some of the women had spent several weeks in in-depth Bible study with her and Sarah. When faced with the overwhelming evidence of what Jesus had done for her, Callie had readily agreed to baptism. Sarah had, too, but much later.

So why did the length of her life as a Christian concern him?

He smiled. "Then we share that in common."

"What does it matter what we share in common?" She motioned to Storm. "He may not live through the day, and Kukara's exhausted. How can you talk about something as trivial as what we have in common?"

"Because our belief in God is not trivial. It is a vital part of our lives." Joshua motioned around the cabin. "Or do you not truly believe?" The hard edge to his voice was unmistakable.

Callie squared her shoulders. "How dare you question my faith. God will never fail me, unlike others who. . .who. . . never mind."

Darkness crossed Joshua's face and she wondered what she had said that caused him to react so. But more important were her own emotions. She might not recall the actual event, but the pain of knowing she had been abandoned was not something she had been able to put behind her. She didn't think she ever would.

"Not everyone betrays a trust intentionally." Joshua studied a section of chinking in the wall that had come loose. "You must have someone on whom you can depend?"

"God is sufficient."

He laid a hand over his heart. "Then I pray that brings you peace. Perhaps someday we can discuss this further." There was a challenge in his voice she could not ignore.

"I am at peace," she assured him.

"Good. I would not be able to stand it if you were not."

Exactly what did he mean by that? Callie started to ask, but he removed his hat and with the fingers of one hand pushed his long wavy hair toward the back of his head. "I am going now," he said. "Call out if you need me. Otherwise, I will check on the boy this evening."

She watched the door in disbelief. He really had gone. When that fact had sunk into her scrambled brain, she swallowed the agony growing inside and turned her mind to Kukara. The woman was now awake and questioning again what would happen to her only child.

It took great strength, but Callie assured her there was nothing else they could do for Storm but pray.

"I will stay with you," she promised.

As time wore on, they talked about Pennsylvania and about how Kukara missed the family she left behind. Callie knew the woman's nervous chatter diverted her mind from worry, so she let Kukara prattle, content to listen with one ear while musing over her conversation with Joshua.

Despite his apparent distaste of her handling of Storm's illness, perhaps he was not such a bad sort. He had responded quickly to her request to tend to Storm, and he had been gentle in his dealings with a distraught Kukara. So why then, at times, did he seem so distant? He spoke to her, but it was never as if he talked *with* her. In the wilds, people relied upon each other for assistance, for survival. Did he not know that?

She decided Joshua Johnston would have to change his ways if he had any plans of remaining with the settlement, and she promptly turned her mind back to Kukara, who was in the middle of asking a question.

The beauty of the Pennsylvania hills was at stake. Callie countered with the idea that this "O-he-yo" land also had some lovely scenery. She had just promised to go on a long hike with Kukara, as soon as Storm was able, when someone pounded at the door.

For a moment her pulse raced as she thought it might be Joshua returning. But the gruff "Open up" could only belong to one person—Levi. Callie hesitated, weighing the consequences of letting him in with Kukara still lying on the bed.

"Company is always welcome," Kukara said, though Callie caught the break in her voice and wondered where the woman found the courage to pretend all was well.

She ignored the black cloud threatening to cover her heart as she pulled the heavy door open. Levi pushed past her into the cabin and cast a basket onto a spindly table before turning to glance around. Three candles sat near each bed, but the light they gave off barely pushed back the darkness. As a result, his face was shaded, making it hard for her to see his expressions.

"What a surprise," Callie managed. "May I ask why you have come?" She sat on the edge of Kukara's bed.

Levi stood in front of the fireplace. The low flames behind him did not illuminate his face, but she sensed he was glaring. "Do you really have to ask? Is it not enough that I have taken the time to fix that?" He nodded toward the basket.

Callie swallowed her retort. This was not the Levi she knew. Her heart slipped into a frightening rhythm, and her hands dampened with sweat. "You apparently are not aware of the severity of Storm's illness," she said. Her gaze slipped cautiously to Storm as she tried to decide which of them needed her protection the most, Kukara or her son.

Levi's eyes narrowed into slits of fiery green as he glared at Storm. "He is sleeping." He pointed at Kukara. "And she looks well enough to handle anything that might crop up."

Behind her, Kukara had pulled herself into a sitting position. She was pale. Callie wanted to dispute Levi, but her own wits were slightly disoriented. She wished Joshua would come back. Now.

What am I thinking? she chided herself. *I do not need Joshua to fight my battles!*

Callie issued a silent prayer before she spoke. "She could become afflicted again at any moment," she insisted. "And Storm is sleeping because Joshua gave him a potion." Her heart quaked at the thought of a different kind of sleep that might overtake Storm if his fever did not break. Could Levi not sense at all what was so vivid in her own mind?

"Suits my plans." Levi started toward her. "If he is asleep, you will not have to worry about him."

He reached out and grabbed Callie's elbow. She tried to wrest her arm from his grasp, but he held tighter. Callused fingers pressed the material of her dress into her skin.

"I will thank you to let me go. Right now."

What was he planning to do? Didn't he remember Kukara and Storm? What if the child awoke and saw them struggling like this?

His grip tightened. "After our picnic, you can do anything you like." He gave her a huge grin, as if the thought of being with him should be her only concern at the moment.

"You are saying that if I go with you, you will let me come back here?" She couldn't believe it could be that easy.

Without realizing it, she had allowed Levi to draw her to her feet. Her stomach churned and her knees wanted to collapse. But that would only serve to let Levi know how weak she felt. And she was not weak! She would handle this as well as she could handle most anything that came along.

"Of course, Callie. What kind of a man do you think I am?" He spoke softly, but cold amusement glittered in his eyes.

"Do not go, Callie," Kukara pleaded weakly.

It was not in her to abandon her patients; they meant too much to her. But if Callie could get Levi out of the cabin, he would be less likely to upset Kukara more than she already was. Which was better? Stand her ground and risk Levi running amok even more than he already had, which by the look in his eyes would not take much, or appease him and go along, hoping nothing would happen that she couldn't control?

Could she handle him if he began to rant and rave? His eyes were hard and dark, and the shadow of a beard he continually tried not to grow haunted his jawline.

She couldn't refuse him, not when his state of mind seemed so tremulous and her own pulse faltered at the idea he might do something horrible to Storm or Kukara. Her chest felt as if a grizzly had sunk his claws into it.

Maintaining a shaky semblance of control, she whispered to Kukara, "Storm is sleeping. You will be fine until I return."

"But. . ." Kukara's concern stretched between them as her gaze slipped to her son.

"He will sleep for a while yet." She issued a silent prayer, only to feel Levi tug on her arm.

"Now." His eyes searched hers, daring her to deny him.

Feeling her world collapse beneath her, she nodded acquiescence. Levi hid the smug look that flitted across his face as he grabbed the basket with one hand and ushered her to the door. Callie stepped off the distance, her heart dragging in her chest. The words to part of the Twenty-third Psalm echoed in her mind: *Yea though I walk through the valley of the shadow of death, I will fear no evil. . . .*

I must trust in God. He will protect me. She took one last look at Kukara before Levi pulled the door closed between them.

❧

Joshua watched as Levi entered the Killbuck cabin. He didn't know Levi well. In fact, he had stayed entirely out of his way since their first meeting—when Levi had made it clear that he intended to wed Callie one day.

Thankfully, there were few at the mission who had been with Brother David in Philadelphia when the Moravians adopted Callie and her sister. So far, Joshua had been able to keep his background, and his earlier relationship with Callie, under wraps.

Joshua had tried to keep his feelings for Callie hidden, but he sensed Levi had figured out there was, or had been, something between them. Joshua didn't like being at odds with anyone and hoped to find a way to ease the tension between Levi and himself.

Telling himself that Levi would hardly dare to cause trouble now with others present, Joshua put the young man out of his mind. It was useless to worry about a situation that he couldn't control. "Give it to God, son," Brother David would say. "He knows what is best."

Lifting his eyes skyward, he passed off this burden to his heavenly Father and then turned toward home. "Home" was a building set aside for the skinning and cleaning of game, but it would do until more cabins were built or until he decided it was time to leave.

Upon reaching the small building, Joshua sat down on the doorstep and attempted to sort out what he should do about Callie. He had been able to deter her from any further questions about Philadelphia, but he sensed it was only a matter of time before she became curious enough to want to know more. After all, if he were in her position, he would be anxious to learn of his life before his loss of memory.

His thoughts turned to the green valleys and rugged mountains he had traversed to find the Moravians, and he was surprised when he heard Brother David's rumbling voice.

"You have no work today?" The elder stretched out a hand in welcome, hitching one hand under a set of suspenders he wore.

"Plenty of it, in fact," Joshua replied. He rose and took the other's hand. "I am only resting until I begin my next round." He spoke calmly, yet his eyes drifted toward the Killbuck home.

"Do you find the work what you expected?" David asked as he settled himself on a tree stump left from clearing the land for the cabins.

"This is what I was meant to do," Joshua affirmed. "Taking care of sickness, chasing death away from the door." While that might be true, there were moments when he knew he would have given it all up if Callie had come through the flood without losing her memory. His desire would have been to be married as swiftly as possible and to go about creating little laughing Johnstons—children he would have taught to love God first, then others, then family. His eyes burned at the thought.

"I have heard good comments from your patients."

"I am glad they are satisfied." Joshua thought of Storm, who might not live. There was nothing else he could do. Did Callie know that? What would happen if they lost the boy? She would blame herself, and he didn't know how anyone could convince her that it was not her fault.

"Joshua? You seem miles away from here. Are you regretting having left Pennsylvania? Perhaps you are not happy with the position you have here?"

Joshua cleared his throat and framed his reply carefully. "I suppose I am the sort who is never satisfied with what I attempt."

Joshua caught movement near the front door of the Killbuck cabin. Callie and Levi. "That is strange," he commented, watching as the couple headed to the fence line across the path from the cabin they had just left.

He told David what had transpired at the cabin and about the condition of Storm when he had left the child just minutes earlier.

David's eyes drifted toward the couple and followed them. "I do not think Callie would leave had she not had a good reason," he assured Joshua. "She is very cautious, that one."

"Yes, well, perhaps I will go check for myself." Joshua could not push away the finger of doubt that nudged his heart.

From everything he had seen, Callie was dedicated. Why then had she apparently deserted her charges? It made no sense. But neither did the man racing across the mission, waving and shouting at Joshua.

Both Joshua and David jerked to their feet just as Abe reached them. His face was white and his breath came in labored gasps. "Suzannah. Time."

six

The seven-foot-high log fence surrounding the mission seemed little protection to Callie as she and Levi walked along beside it. The hewn wood gave off a sticky-sweet smell, and nettles grabbed at the hem of her skirt. Overhead, clouds covered the sun. The usual bird sounds were missing, lending the day a depressing air that matched her disposition.

Callie and Levi had made it almost to the far end of the fence, where it disappeared into the woods, before she dared ask where they were going.

"The spring." He was walking behind her or, rather, pushing her ahead of him. His hand gripped her elbow with brute strength, and his voice seemed to blast away at her with the sureness of an expert hunter's aim.

She leveled her shuddering shoulders and forced herself to take a deep breath. She had feared he would take her somewhere else, like toward the river, where people seldom ventured. At least the spring was visited frequently. And though she would be embarrassed if someone discovered them there, embarrassment was secondary to safety—she wanted them to be found.

She was upset at the way Levi barged into the cabin and demanded that she accompany him, but doing as he asked had seemed the lesser of two evils at the time. But now that she was here. . .

At that moment, Levi slid into place beside her, and she gave him a quick sideways glance. His green eyes were darker than normal, his red hair more unruly than she had ever seen it. His jaw was clenched and the lines around his eyes seemed more apparent than ever. A muscle jumped along the side of his neck.

Callie had heard talk among the men at the mission about the French and British soldiers and what they were likely to do if they continued to press westward in search of more land and more furs. She had grown to dislike those who might uproot what she had been striving to attain: freedom and peace.

With Levi holding her arm as if he did not trust her, the same feeling stormed her heart. Peace and freedom seemed like butterflies that had escaped their cocoons and forgotten to land somewhere. Regardless of all she had been taught about a woman's place in the world, no man had the right to treat a woman like this!

"Quit dragging your feet," Levi admonished her as she attempted to summon the courage to question him.

"I did not realize I was," she muttered in apology, not caring how insincere she sounded. The look in his eyes made it clear that to disobey would place her in even more jeopardy.

Levi peered at her from beneath uneven brows, looking like a hawk ready to swoop upon some hapless field mouse. She tried not to stare at the angry slash of his lips, for they only frightened her more.

"You were," he snapped.

I must go along with him, she told herself. She knew he was the sort that liked to be in charge, to have everything his own way.

"Then I will walk faster." She hoped this would pacify him and checked to see his reaction.

The whites of his eyes flared as if he suspected she was ready to bolt. Callie wondered if she had said the wrong thing. The last time she had seen him like this had been when an albino deer hide he had brought back on a hunt had been ruined. He had spent a week ranting about the carelessness of the young Delaware Levi had entrusted with helping him preserve the skin. Despite Brother David's interference, the young boy had been devastated by Levi's reaction and now stayed as far away from him as possible. Levi did not allow anyone to speak of it now, preferring that the episode be forgotten.

The dreary thought crossed her mind that this might be a similar incident, one she might have to work at forgetting. Callie recalled the hate showing on his face during the first few days after the hide had been ruined. She had no wish to see Levi repeat the horrible lack of common sense he had exhibited then. For that reason, she renewed her silent vow to do whatever she could to please him.

He stepped up the pace and she stumbled, her shorter legs no match for Levi's long, powerful ones. He just clutched her arm tighter, as if he thought it might encourage her to be more obedient.

Distaste settled in her mouth as they neared the glen. At first glance, it appeared to be a perfect spot for a couple to enjoy time together. It was heavily shaded, and some of the trees dipped their branches into the stream as it coursed over a rock shelf in a pleasant waterfall. In a pond at the bottom of the waterfall, water babbled over rounded stones the settlers called "river biscuits."

"We are here." Levi's announcement was unnecessary.

Callie's knees weakened at the peril she heard in his voice. She tried to move out of his grasp and settle onto a boulder, but before she could, Levi grabbed both arms and spun her around. He stared into her eyes then drew her against his chest.

His breath escaped his mouth in hot, short blasts, while he held her with terrifying force. Her ability to breathe seemed lost somewhere between her head and her lungs. She wanted to push him away, but his arms clutched her close.

Callie closed her eyes. If she didn't look, it wasn't happening. She had never been in this position. It was not allowed of those who were unmarried.

Levi relaxed his crushing hold but did not free her. His hands encircled her slender forearms like the chains she had once seen on slaves destined for a Southern plantation.

"Please. Do not." She was embarrassed that she had to plead, but if it would break the spell he seemed to be under, she would do anything.

Levi's chuckle drifted across her cheek. "I am not going to hurt you."

"Good," she whispered.

He draped one arm casually across her shoulder and pursed his lips while staring down into her eyes.

Regardless of how quickly he had composed himself, Callie didn't trust him. She wanted to be away from him, back at the mission where there were good, proper men like Brother David and Joshua. Her mind bounced around trying to form a plan.

Eat. Escape. Head home.

Perhaps she should scream and hope someone heard? But who would? The spring was a good half-mile from the western edge of Schoenbrunn. No one but Kukara even knew she had left the mission.

Levi released her without warning and she stumbled back a step. Indignant at his treatment, Callie recovered her balance and tilted her chin up, jamming her hands on her hips as she did.

"You have made a mistake, Levi." Her chest heaved with exertion, pain, and mistrust. Once those words were out of her mouth, she felt slightly more assured that she might be able to control what was happening. If she could keep him off balance, perhaps he would forget what he intended.

"Mistake?" He appeared confused as he lowered his head toward his chest, but he kept his eyes locked with hers. "I do not think so," he jeered, but his arm fell away from her shoulder.

The lessening of the bond between them freed her. "I do," she stormed uncharacteristically. "You are treating me as if I am a common bed jumper, like. . .like those women we met on the way from Pennsylvania."

The thought of those disgusting women made her physically sick. Ever since his family joined the Moravians, three and a half years earlier, Levi had claimed to be a God-fearing Christian. But the look in his eyes and the way he had drawn her to his chest made her wonder if perhaps she really didn't know him after all. How strong had his faith been on that trip a year ago?

Levi shoved a hand through his riotous curls and reached out toward her cheek. She swallowed hard.

"I know you are not one of those, Callie. You are uncommon. Can you not see I love you?"

She felt as if someone were pushing her over a cliff and she had no way to keep from falling. He loved her. No! Love was not supposed to happen like this. Love was soft and quiet, strong and gentle, not pushy and blustering.

Fury built inside her. She repressed it. One of them had to maintain control emotionally. It must be her, since Levi did not appear to be thinking straight.

"You have a strange way of showing your love," she protested. Even the few steps she put between them did not lessen the feeling that he was squeezing the very life out of her.

"You are so busy taking care of the sick, what else could I do?" A little-boy-lost look softened his features.

A momentary surge of sorrow for him surprised her. Then she recalled how he had treated her—barging into the home of her patients and sweeping her away.

"You did not have to force me." Her voice carried throughout the glen. She wished someone would find them, despite the fact that there would be gossip later. Anything was preferable to standing here looking at his eyes of flint.

"You are right." He kicked at a rock and watched it scamper into the brush.

She was relieved he might have come to his senses, that escape might be within reach. A sense of determination pressed her next words from her. "You act as if I am a trinket to play with," she began before stopping abruptly.

How far could she go and not upset him? Strangely, she didn't care. She wanted him to understand she was not someone he could push around at his whims.

"I am a human being, Levi. I have feelings. I have dreams. What you did was not proper." She hugged her arms around her waist. She had never felt so desolate.

In the distance, a mockingbird called out to its mate. Levi moved away from her and threw a hand across his brow. The basket lay on the ground between them. When he had dropped it, a loaf of bread had fallen out. A sparrow flitted around as if trying to decide whether or not to land and attempt to eat it.

Callie watched the bird instead of glaring at Levi. Here she was, struggling to hold her temper and to get away from Levi, while one of God's creatures was taking time out to find its next meal. If what was happening to her was not so momentous, she would break into demented laughter. Perhaps she would anyway and see how he reacted. The thought soothed her jangling nerves.

"Survival belongs to the fit," Joshua had told her that first night when she had known only enough to call him "Magicworker." Where was he now? Tending to the sick while she was here, fighting to survive. Callie was overcome by the desire to rant at Joshua for leaving her alone in the cabin without making sure she was safe. No, she told herself sharply, her safety was no concern of Joshua's, no matter how often her mind turned to him lately.

Levi took a step toward her, his arms stretched out in front of him menacingly. Her breath rasped in the back of her throat. A thousand different images flashed through her mind.

She saw herself fleeing without facing the threat, turning tail and running as fast as she could. How many times in the last few years had she allowed the relationship between them to progress against her will? And where had that passiveness gotten her?

Callie kept a wary eye on every movement Levi made while she considered what to do next. She had to make him see what he was doing, not just because she was furious with him for acting so foolishly, but because she needed to make sure she could stand up to him and survive. For all she knew, in the past she may have been as timid as a field mouse hiding from a night owl in search of its supper.

Callie decided at that moment that no man was going to tell her what she would or would not do. For if he did, she would lose the new self she had worked on becoming since the flood swept away her past.

She ground her teeth together and glared at him. She would not allow Levi to make her feel insignificant.

"Did you hear what I said?" she prodded.

Levi didn't answer right away. Instead, he straightened and looked as if he were considering how they had come to be standing here so at odds with each other. Confusion glittered in his eyes briefly, then was replaced by something Callie could not define.

"I am not a trinket to play with," she repeated, more for her benefit than his. The words were a small comfort, coming as they did in such a meek tone.

She cleared her throat. Birds quarreled in the distance, forming an apt backdrop to what was going on here. The sun peeked through the heavy tree cover, warming her skin. The damp earth around the spring emitted a rank odor that wafted around her.

"I heard." His voice had changed. Gone was the malice she had heard earlier. Now there was gentleness and remorse. She could almost believe he was the old Levi she had known not long ago.

The Bible spoke of people doing strange things because evil had inhabited their bodies. Was it possible Levi's actions were directed by demons? No, she would not believe that. Levi alone was accountable for his behavior. And because he seemed so skittish, she must remain polite and courteous. Not to mention determined to find a way out of this without damaging her virtue, which she suddenly felt was what he intended.

"I will not mention this to anyone," she offered, her pulse pounding in her ears. There was no going back now.

Levi didn't answer for a moment. He took advantage of her discomfort to cross one ankle over the other and dig the toe of one boot into the ground. He stared at her as if seeing her for the first time. His expression clouded and he pounded a clenched fist against the side of his leg.

"I am so sorry, Callie," he said heavily. He ran a hand through the too-long curls on the back of his neck. "I only wanted to see you. Will you forgive me?"

She glanced up at the clouds gathering in the sky; they now covered the sun. Shadows filled the glade and Callie's soul. She had known Levi long enough to know something was making him behave this way. But what?

She wanted to forgive him, wanted him to be the old Levi, but she also wanted him to know he could not treat a woman, or any human, in such a way.

It took an enormous effort for her to speak. "I will work on doing that, Levi." Her tone hardly conveyed earnestness. She watched him, sure he would advance toward her again.

When Levi did nothing but stare off into the trees, she blew a sharp breath between her teeth. What was he thinking? Was he planning how to retract everything he had done? She didn't know. But she did know one thing—she was going to get away.

Levi had crossed an invisible line in their relationship.

There was no going back, no going forward, not for them. Callie glanced back only once as she pushed aside a branch to begin her trek. Despite a racing pulse, she refused to run. Running was a sign of weakness, and she was not weak. Nevertheless, she had to force her feet not to hurry.

❧

Inside the Solomon cabin, surrounded by a quilt damp with perspiration and tears, Suzannah sat upright, her hands wrapped around her abdomen. Joshua took one swift look at the woman and knew she had waited too long to send for his help. Regardless of what he had said to Callie two weeks ago, he was not sure either of the twins would survive. He calculated they were at least two months early. He had learned in medical training that single births sometimes had a chance at this stage, but a double birth? Very unlikely.

"Go get Callie." His command was intended to occupy Abe without unduly upsetting him. He described where he had last seen her headed and sent the disconsolate man on his way.

"Make it stop!" Suzannah wailed in an eerie repetition of two short weeks ago.

"We have no choice." How he wished there were some way to soften the words! He had grown up in the orphanage his parents ran, among those who had no family. His mother had always insisted that no matter what his station in life, he was to be compassionate for and understanding of those less fortunate. Yet no matter how many times he faced death or disaster, it never became easy.

Suzannah raised pain-filled, defeated eyes to meet his. "You have to! They will not live if they come now!"

They? Callie must have told her to expect twins again.

"We shall see." He patted her arm gently. "I cannot give you any more of the potion."

Suzannah produced a strip of rawhide that she bit into savagely during the worst of her pains. She twisted the thin piece of leather over and over. "I will do it if it will save my children," she begged.

He wished it were that easy—to simply administer another dose and forget the consequences. He could do it, he knew, and if something happened to her, who would be the wiser? It would be thought an accident, and Suzannah would become just another casualty of the cruel wilderness. He could leave the mission to find a new life, a new woman, a new home.

Joshua shook his head. He was not cut from secondhand cloth. His mother had also seen to that.

"You can have no more because I am not sure what will happen if we continue to use it," he said. A sudden burst of remorse flowed through him. If he had stayed in Philadelphia and finished his medical training, he would have learned more about the drug's effects. He had always thought things through before acting on them. Except this time, when finding the woman he loved had proved more important than anything else.

And now he was trying to save two infants who would probably not survive and a woman who was the closest friend of the woman he loved, Callie. And she didn't remember him.

"I am willing to risk it." Suzannah's voice was strong despite the pain and heartache written across her pinched face.

"I am not." Joshua shoved his sleeves up above his elbows, conscious of the ragged scar that ran down his forearm. "There is no telling what could happen to you or the babies if we continued."

He moved to the fireplace where water simmered in a kettle, stirred the embers, and added a log before returning to Suzannah.

She seemed to realize there was nothing she could do to convince him otherwise. "Get Callie," she whimpered.

"Abe has already gone for her." At least he could appease her on that.

"She will help me," Suzannah insisted. "You stay away."

ﷺ

Coming through a gap between homes, Callie caught sight of Abe. Her heart fell at the look on his face. She grabbed the sides of her long skirt and rushed toward the cabin, a prayer beating in her heart. *Please, God, more time.*

She tore through the partially open door, heedless of the fact that she had left Abe standing outside. Her eyes quickly appraised the situation.

As she did, she felt Joshua's gaze rake over her. Callie gave him an accusatory stare in return, one that demanded to know why he had not worked his healing again.

He continued to look at her through dark, brooding eyes. His lips were a slash across the beard stubble on his face, and even the smattering of freckles on his nose seemed subdued. She supposed he would somehow place the blame for Suzannah's predicament on her, just as he would also point the finger at her for Storm's dilemma.

Suzannah growled, a deep, agonizing sound that drew Callie to her friend's side. She whispered encouraging words that she knew Suzannah would not hear. She had to say them in order to fill her own mind with thoughts of things other than what she could not change.

"Now." Joshua's command came from behind her.

Before she could properly settle into position, there was an infant in her hands, a girl with dusky red hair. Sophie Ruth, Callie thought, knowing the names Suzannah and Abe had picked out for the twins once they were over the shock of learning there would be two again. The birth cord was wrapped around the baby's neck and she was a horrible blue.

One of them. . . Joshua's prediction came out of nowhere and slammed into Callie. This was what he had meant. That one of them would not live!

Callie gritted her teeth, determined to show him how much

he knew. She stared into the lifeless eyes of the tiny babe, willing her to take a breath. Nothing. The infant lay like a piece of driftwood against her arm. A wave of weariness engulfed her, but she was not about to give up.

Again and again she petitioned God to allow Sophie to breathe. Time ceased to exist. She had been so determined that Suzannah and Abe would have two infants to replace the two little girls they had already lost.

"The second one," Joshua barked.

She wanted to scream, "No. I am not ready."

A glance at Sophie Ruth lying across her forearm, her color no better, her life over before it had begun, brought a bitter taste to her mouth. But Suzannah's shriek brought her back to the task at hand.

I must be strong, she told herself.

Quickly, reverently, she wrapped Sophie Ruth in a blanket before laying the infant gently on the end of the bed. It took all the determination she could muster to turn around. Joshua was watching her again. He had positioned himself near Suzannah's head and was patting her brow with a damp cloth. His hair fell in disarray, partially covering his shaggy eyebrows. He gave Callie a tight smile, which shored up her nerves, and she turned back to await the next infant.

Hannah Grace had none of the sickly pallor of her twin. She came out kicking, her lungs filling with air and her lusty cry breaking the tension in the room, reminding Callie that her own despair must wait. But the joy of hearing Hannah Grace did not remove the stain of Sophie Ruth's death from her heart. She would carry that pain with her forever.

Callie looked back and forth from Suzannah to the precious infant in Callie's arms who nuzzled against her. Frightened at the jumble of emotions within her chest, Callie abruptly held the baby away from her.

Joshua had coaxed Suzannah into lying back and she was

reaching out with both hands, fingers fully extended, eyes full of tears, searching for her babies.

Hot drops stung Callie's eyes as she handed the squirming infant to her mother.

"Hannah Grace," Suzannah cooed, sensing this was the second child she had delivered. She snuggled the infant tightly against her breast. While the weary woman stared into the barely open eyes of her daughter, Callie brushed away tears that slipped down her cheeks.

Joshua moved toward Callie, a handmade quilt dangling from his fingers. "There was nothing you could do," he said.

Callie glanced at Sophie Ruth, a still, silent bundle on the end of the bed. A fresh round of tears threatened to overtake her.

"How can you say that?" Pain slashed her soul for the grief Suzannah would carry with her for years. Two brown patches of dirt would become three.

"Because if it had not been for your care in the beginning, she would not have made it this far." His voice became so low she had to strain to hear him.

Callie wanted to believe him. She *ached* to believe him. But it had been Joshua that night who had spoken the enigmatic words, "One of them. . ." Why hadn't she pursued his meaning? Knowing his thoughts, no matter how speculative, might have helped prepare her for this grief that wrenched her heart.

She jerked away from the bed, crossed to the fireplace, and hugged herself, hoping to stem the fresh round of tears that stormed her cheeks. *He must not see me cry,* she said silently. She didn't ask herself why that was important. It just was.

From across the room, she heard Suzannah's shaky voice ask, "The other one? Sophie Ruth or Isaac Daniel?"

Callie bit her bottom lip until she noticed the taste of blood on her tongue. She had no words to tell Suzannah she had lost another child. She couldn't even recall what she had said last time this had happened. Desperately she flicked her eyes heavenward, hoping the heavenly Father would assist her in her time of need.

"Do you not know," Joshua began, "that 'in heaven their angels do always behold the face of my Father'?"

His calm, gentle voice softened the edge of her grief as she recognized the words were from Matthew, chapter eighteen, verse ten. But she felt Suzannah's torment as Joshua continued. In phrase after phrase he talked about the wonders of heaven, the golden streets, the freedom. "No tears fall there," he whispered. "There will be only joy and reunion with our loved ones."

Callie sought solace in staring at his dusty boots. She wondered how she would ever face Suzannah and Abe again. She had failed them terribly. Joshua was now gently informing Suzannah of the truth, but someone would have to tell Abe. And the grandparents. And the rest of the mission. Who would do it? Callie? Never. She had done that once before and she would never forget it.

Callie's shoulders shook as she understood the burden God had given her. She would have to do it. A stranger should not be asked to do something of such significance. It was her place, her responsibility.

She stared down absently and only realized after a few moments that a pair of boots had come into view, obstructing her view of the straw covering the floor.

Her name came to her as a whisper. Then she felt his fingers gently nudge her chin upward so that her gaze would meet his. Bright blooms of color burst upon her cheeks, but she was unaware of that as she lost herself in the solitude of eyes bluer than an April sky after the rain.

Silent messages passed between them, as if they were two souls who had found a way to communicate without speaking. She felt her fears subside.

They stood like that for an eternity, each willing the other not to speak about what had just happened between them. Joshua's fingers rested just behind her chin in a soft hollow she had not been aware of before now. Tiny ribbons of enjoyment raced through her. . .until she remembered the woman lying on the bed behind them.

What was she doing? Her pulse raced. Her hands were damp, her insides churning. What power in the universe had led them to this? Callie pushed away the curious feeling that left her insides turned upside down. No matter how much she wanted to continue exploring the craggy features of his face, no matter what his touch had done to her, she could not forget he knew things about her that she didn't remember. That frightened her more than anything else.

❧

Joshua stood aside and gave Callie time to grieve with Suzannah. It had been reckless of him to reach out and touch her, but he had not been able to will away the desire to do so. It was becoming increasingly difficult to fight what came naturally to him: the desire to take care of the person he loved above all else. The fact that she didn't know the depth of his feelings only made it more difficult to appear detached.

He studied her, his gaze lingering on her fragile shoulders and the tendrils of slightly blond hair that had crept out from under her bonnet. How the Calliope he had known had changed. She was no longer a carefree young girl. She was Callie, woman of the wilderness, helper to those in pain.

He ached to hold her against him, to feel the strength of her heartbeat. But how could he? She had no idea what they had planned years ago. And he had no right to tell her, to drop it in her lap like a too-hot potato. No, he had promised David he would bide his time and wait. And he would pray she would remember who he was, who she was, what they had been to each other. And no matter what, he would carry with him forever the memory of her soft brown eyes staring into his as if she remembered every vow they had ever made to each other.

Abe's rap at the door interrupted Joshua's misery. Joshua admitted him, feeling useless as the rangy man bent in sorrow by his wife's bedside.

Joshua heard Callie explain about the loss, his admiration for her bravery growing as she did so. It seemed that only a few moments passed before she joined him at the table. Her petite oval face was flushed, her eyes fringed with crimson, clearly a result of her grief. Again Joshua wanted to touch her, to assure himself that five years of waiting was over.

"I must thank you," Callie said after she settled onto a chair. She used both hands to smudge away the tears she had cried as she spoke with Abe.

"It is you who deserves the credit," he replied. He was amazed at her ability to put aside her pain and attend to those who needed her compassion. Without thinking, he reached out and squeezed her hand, suddenly realizing that her reaction would likely be shock.

Callie didn't pull away. She only looked at him with huge dark eyes. She was the most beautiful woman he had ever known, but he was sure she viewed him through eyes of friendship, not love, something he was powerless to change. After arriving at the mission, he had learned she was expected to wed Levi. Joshua didn't care for the situation, but he would not damage what she and Levi had established together.

As if uncomfortable with his gaze, Callie abruptly stood and went over to the hearth, where she prodded the embers of the fire. When she turned back, he was gone.

seven

"We will be all right," Abe said, nudging Callie toward the door. "Love will see us through."

Before leaving, she gave Suzannah one last look. Then, finding words insufficient, Callie closed the door behind her and walked out into the bright sunshine.

At home, she prayed God would be with the Solomons during this tragic time. Thoroughly drained, she collapsed into a rocking chair in the corner and that was how Sarah found her.

"I am so sorry, Callie," her sister said, resting her hand on Callie's shoulder. "I heard about. . .the babies."

Callie rubbed at her eyes before answering. "I. . .we did all we could, but there was nothing. . ." Her voice caught and she raised tear-filled eyes to Sarah. Why did she have to go through this again? More importantly, why did Abe and Suzannah? What was the purpose in giving life if it was to be snuffed out before it could begin?

Sarah patted her shoulder. "You do not have to talk about it. I know how you felt the last time this happened."

Callie threw both hands over her face. "I do not know that I can ever talk about this. There is too much pain. . ."

The pain was not only due to losing Sophie Ruth; it also was caused by Levi's ungentlemanly behavior at the Killbuck cabin and the spring.

"I am sorry. It must sound lacking, but that is all I can say." Sarah rubbed her arms. "I will light a fire. Perhaps the warmth will cheer us up."

"There is no fire on earth that can take away death's chill, Sarah."

"I know that," Sarah rejoined, but she moved toward the hearth anyway, keeping her face turned away from her sister.

Melancholy hung over them for the rest of the afternoon. Sarah tried her best to lighten the mood with bits of news she had picked up. She mentioned Storm, in case it might shock Callie into remembering that life must go on.

"I stopped by the Killbucks'," Sarah said, her voice firm and steady. "Storm is still weak and feverish."

"Then there is no change?" Callie didn't know why she had asked. She hadn't expected there to be, but she hoped.

"No, none. Your Joshua came by while I was there."

"He is not my Joshua!" She should have been the one to check on the boy, not him. A fresh round of despair moved through her.

Sarah nodded. "Whatever you say. He administered another potion and said to tell you not to worry about going there tonight; he will take care of Storm."

"How nice." Callie's words were laced with irritation. He had brushed her off without any regard to her involvement. For a few days she had forgotten that in the beginning she had thought he had come to take her position away from her. Now that concern resurfaced.

"Yes, it was thoughtful of him," Sarah went on. "We had a little chat and then Levi walked me home."

"Levi picked you up?" Shock propelled her words from her mouth.

Sarah clucked her tongue. "It was harmless, Callie. All he did was walk me home."

Sarah might think it harmless, but Callie was concerned. She must tell her sister about the way Levi had behaved that morning. But how? Sarah would no doubt take it the wrong way and point out that Levi was apparently becoming bored waiting for Callie to decide to wed him.

"I am glad you had an escort," she finally said.

"That is all it was. No harm in that, is there?"

"No." Callie clasped her hands in front of her. What was Levi up to? And why couldn't she just tell Sarah about what he had done that morning?

Sarah and Levi? She could not let that happen! Sarah was sixteen and had no idea of the intricacies of a man-woman relationship. And Levi, hunter-lean Levi whose actions this morning had proven to her once and for all that she could never stand beside him as his wife. . .what was he up to? She had plainly told him not to count on her for any future relationship. Any chance for closeness between them was now gone.

But Sarah? How quickly he may have switched his allegiance after the fiasco at the spring.

Sarah's brows narrowed and a quizzical expression appeared on her face; it was as if she could read Callie's thoughts. "You must be tired. I promised MaryBeth I would come see her, so I had better be going."

"Sarah?" Callie began, deciding she must at least warn her sister to be careful.

"Yes?" Sarah turned and gazed at Callie with such innocence, Callie found she could not speak.

Perhaps if she just stood back and watched, things would work themselves out. "Be careful," she finally said.

"I always am," Sarah replied.

The day's events had drained Callie emotionally, and as she recalled them, her heart surged with renewed grief. Thoughts of the little blue infant would not leave her. The tears she had been fighting for most of the day filled her eyes. This time she did not try to stem the flow.

❧

"We could not save both," Joshua explained to Brother David across the table. He had sought out David after leaving the Solomons' cabin and checking on Storm.

"It is sad when we lose a soul, especially when the soul is untried," David commented.

"Sophie Ruth is with Jesus."

David nodded. "Yes, but we must not forget the parents. Their road has been paved with loss." He wiped at the corners of his eyes. "They have one they can hold, but the memories of the others will always walk with them."

"It is hard to lose someone you love," he agreed. Joshua had never lost a child, but he had lost Callie.

David removed his ever-present Bible from under his arm and laid it on his lap. "How are things between you and Callie?"

The only thing Joshua had left was the open wound of an aching heart. "I am not sure I can continue this way," he admitted.

"I do not believe that," David replied. "You waited five years for this and now you have changed your mind?"

"I do not know." Joshua jumped up and began to pace.

David settled back in his chair. "You are the only one who does know, Joshua. Are you telling me you are giving up?"

Was he? David had told him Levi and Callie had planned to wed someday. Where would that information lead him?

"I am not giving up. I just never imagined how difficult this would be when I decided not to tell her who I really am. And you have enlightened me as to Levi's expectations for her," he added.

"I will not preach to you, Joshua, but sometimes we make decisions that seem entirely wrong. We must trust God to work out any good that can come of them."

"So you do not believe I am wrong?" The question gouged a canyon in his heart. He did not really need David's approval. He had made his decision long ago to find Callie and pursue the promise they had made, despite the obstacles that might entail.

David cocked his head to one side. "You still believe she will look at you and remember who you are and who she is, do you not?"

"Yes. Well, I—"

"I will say this," David interjected. "At the risk of sounding pessimistic, I do not think that will happen. She has come a long way. She has risen above challenges that would have made many strong men turn tail and run. She lost her parents and then she lost her home at the orphanage. And if that were not enough, Callie followed me to this lonely piece of wilderness." David crossed his arms.

"It was not as if she had much of a choice, David," Joshua said. "I was there. She did not know who she was. You offered safety. What else could she have done?"

David studied him silently. Long moments passed. Finally, with a look of exasperation on his face, the elder offered his opinion. "Have you considered why she did it? I think in her heart she thought it would distance her from what had happened."

Joshua mulled over David's words. "You sound as if you have spoken with her about this."

David shook his head. "It is in everything she does. She is gentle and patient with children, yet she never gets too close to them. She loves being around elderly people, yet she does not socialize with them much. She is happiest when she is alone, or with Sarah; but she gives freely of herself to any needy person in our midst. Do I have to tell you why?"

"She sees them as outcasts from their former homes also," Joshua mused. "Since God loves them, she believes no one but He can accept her for what she is since she does not know who she was."

David nodded. "Everyone here expects her to marry Levi someday, but I do not think so. The man who marries Callie will be the one who can help her build new memories." He paused and glanced into Joshua's eyes. "He will show her that yesterday does not matter. Above all, he will accept her for who she is now, not who she was before."

Joshua stared out the window. He loved that woman. But was it the Calliope he had known in the orphanage or the Callie he had found here in the wilderness that his heart longed for?

"You were not worried about her when she went to the spring with Levi because you trusted her judgment," Joshua reflected.

Why hadn't he realized that before? Because he had been too caught up in seeing her with Levi that all he could think of was the worst—that she had deserted Kukara and Storm.

David leaned forward, keeping his arms crossed in front of him in the manner Joshua was learning meant the elder had something important to say. "I knew Callie would do the right thing. What about you, Joshua?"

≥•

It was all Callie could do to roll out of bed after a restless night. Her stomach was queasy and every muscle between her neck and her ankles ached. In fact, her entire body felt as if it were a piece of buckskin that had been stewed in hot water all night long.

Without waking Sarah, she visited those who were ill, then returned home, preferring the silent condemnation of the log chinking to facing well-meaning men and women who would want to talk about Sophie Ruth and how sorry they were she and Joshua had not been able to save the infant.

Escape was not that easy. Even after she had returned home and flopped on her bed, her mind kept revisiting what had happened yesterday. The incident with Levi. Then Sophie Ruth. Hannah Grace. Suzannah's wail of grief. And when those memories had played themselves out, the image of Joshua kept coming back to her. Joshua bravely explaining to Suzannah about Sophie Ruth. Joshua touching Callie's hand in friend-ship, looking at her across the table through those endless blue eyes, eyes she had compared to the color of a lake just a few short weeks ago when he had first joined them at the mission.

Then, she had thought him mysterious, perhaps intent on taking her position away from her. But after watching him as he worked with her fellow villagers, Callie knew there was nothing mysterious about Joshua. He was kind and more than willing to share what he had with those who had little. He did everything he could to ease a person's pain.

So where did that leave her? Since the day she asked him where he was from, Joshua had avoided any further conversa-tion about the orphanage or why she should remember him. But at the Solomons' cabin, when he sat across from her and reached for her hand, she had felt something stir between them. Something unfamiliar. Something bothersome. It made her wonder if there had ever been anything between them. . . .

Callie shook her head. She was thinking like Sarah, imag-ining things that weren't there. She was just worn out from all that had happened.

"You do not know how to relax," Sarah had told her a few months ago. She had been running back and forth to almost every home in the mission, trying to prevent a round of influenza from taking root and wiping out half of the mis-sion's population. "Take some time and just be yourself."

Callie wanted to, but she didn't know who she was supposed to be, apart from someone who tended to Schoenbrunn's ill. The only thing she knew about herself was that she was a castoff her parents had not wanted. Brother David and the others at the mission didn't see her that way. It was her viewpoint, but a view so firmly ingrained that it was all she knew. If her own parents had not wanted her, then why would anyone? There was only God, the supreme being of total understanding.

Frustrated, Callie clenched her fists, then let her hands drop into her lap. How would she ever find out who she had been? Joshua. His name erupted into her consciousness like an answer to prayer.

He knows. He can tell me. Her pulse beat out the words and battered them against her heart. Callie shoved them away. From all appearances, he did not like talking about those days in Pennsylvania. And it was not proper, no matter how much she wanted to know, for her to demand he tell her what he knew.

Callie felt as if she were trapped in a circle, the questions bouncing around in her head until the only thing she could think of was that somehow, some way, she must convince Joshua to explain what he knew about her.

"You awake?" Sarah called.

Lost in her own thoughts, Callie hadn't heard her sister slip across the room. *I must not let Sarah know what I have been thinking,* she thought as she rolled over and opened one eye halfway.

"I have already done my rounds. For now, I am going to rest. Yesterday took a lot out of me."

A look of surprise crossed Sarah's face. "What about morning service?"

"I am not going anywhere," Callie explained.

"Not even to Sophie Ruth's funeral?" Sarah asked.

"Just let me sleep," she answered. She turned away, hoping Sarah would not probe for her reason.

Sarah patted her shoulder as she was apt to do when she had no words with which to reply, then puttered around the cabin until Callie heard her leave for the morning worship.

Try as she might, with Sarah gone, Callie could not avoid the cabin's silence pressing in on her. In the past when she faced a tragedy, she had done so alone. Since she had found God, she had sincerely tried to allow Him to take her burdens and show her the answer. Sometimes, though, she felt it took God too long to reveal His will.

She had Sarah, and though they were natural sisters, she had never felt as close as she thought sisters should be. The seven-year age difference was one thing, but Callie also suspected it was due to the fact they had been kept separate at the orphanage.

The whoosh of a tree branch against the outside wall jerked her away from what was quickly becoming a depressing line of thought.

"Callie? Coming in. Stay where you are."

Ruth Lyons's voice preceded the tiny woman into the room. Ruth was Levi and Suzannah's mother. Her gray-silver hair was covered by the bonnet common among the Moravians. Age lines around her eyes drew attention to sullen smudges beneath them. The dress she wore was tattered and much patched, typical of a frontier woman.

"Sarah mentioned at worship that you were not feeling well. I have come to sit with you." Ruth breezed across the small room.

Callie had known Ruth the entire time she had been with the Moravians. Ruth would go out of her way to make others feel better. Callie knew she had no choice but to submit to the woman's ministrations. She motioned Ruth to have a seat as she pushed herself up and leaned her back against the wall that served as her bed's headboard.

For the first few moments, Ruth made small talk, as if hesitant to bring up the subject of the twins. Then Callie watched helplessly as Ruth shoved a hand against her mouth and sobs poured forth.

No one blamed Callie or Joshua, Ruth insisted. They were all thankful one infant had survived.

Callie shifted position, trying to ignore her exhaustion. "Is there anything I can do?"

Ruth seemed to measure how ill Callie looked. "Levi is worried about you," she commented.

"Tell him thank you." Callie wanted to ask if Levi had said that or if it was just Ruth trying to make her feel better. Ruth didn't know what Levi had done, and Callie was not about to raise that subject. Memories of that ugly episode and the baby's death hung around her heart like a dead weight.

"He is digging the grave," Ruth added. Her voice caught at the end, but she did not break her gaze with Callie.

Callie tried to keep her distance when small children were lost. This one, though, seemed to have destroyed her resolve.

She asked again what she could do to help.

Ruth's lips trembled. "Pray for Suzannah," she said. "And. . ." She glanced around the cabin as if she expected to find someone there listening. "And stand with us—with our family—tomorrow at the cemetery."

A hollow feeling settled in Callie's stomach and a roar filled her ears. "Is there not something else I could do?" Callie asked. Standing with them, hurting with them, watching as they lowered the tiny body into the earth. How could she do that?

Ruth patted her hand. "It would mean so much to us, to Suzannah," she added. The look in her eyes ripped Callie's heart and made her feel even worse.

"I will think about it," Callie murmured.

"I must go check on Levi and then to Suzannah's." Ruth gathered her skirt folds and brushed Callie's cheek with a kiss.

Callie watched the humble woman leave and realized she was relieved that other than to ask her to stand with them at the burial service, Ruth hadn't really spoken much about the infants.

She dozed off until Sarah returned from MaryBeth's. They passed the rest of the day carding wool and kneading bread, being careful not to talk about Sophie Ruth. After eating, Callie began to feel better physically, and Sarah caught her up on the goings-on at the mission, at least the ones important to her young mind.

Callie's weariness returned by evening and her meal consisted of a slice of bread with butter on it. Her arms and legs felt as if she had been dragged for miles by a horse-drawn wagon; and as soon as she lay on her bed, she fell into a deep sleep.

It seemed she had no more than closed her eyes before she was awake again. Dawn's soft light had climbed the yellowed paper covering the one window. In the distance she could hear the familiar crows of roosters welcoming the day.

Swinging her legs over the bedside, she wished she had not awakened so early, as it only gave her more time to decide if she would go to the funeral. She had no real reason to stay home. The nausea she had experienced yesterday had passed and all that remained was bone-weary despair.

Callie's subconscious pleaded with her to remember what Suzannah must be feeling. In the end, the thought of her closest friend saying farewell to another child convinced her she must go. She would stand with the family as Ruth had asked, regardless of the pain she felt herself.

eight

"Your eyes look sad," Sarah commented as they made their way north on the hard-packed dirt trail to the cemetery called God's Acres.

"Thanks for not mentioning how red they are," Callie replied. Once she was up and about, she had spent the morning crying for Suzannah and the children she had borne but never had the opportunity to love.

She didn't know which was worse, losing a child or losing your parents. It was a question she had often asked over the last few years. *How can you mourn what you cannot remember having?* she often scolded herself as she lay tossing and turning in her bed.

She glanced down at the dreary gray dress she wore. It seemed to mirror the low clouds that encompassed as much of the sky as she could see and was even plainer than normal today without its slash-of-white bib that she had taken off as a sign of mourning.

She joined the quiet crowd gathered around the tiny wound in the earth. Most of them wiped at their eyes periodically and sent short glances down the path as they waited for the grieving parents to arrive.

For lack of anything better to do, Callie took the opportunity to examine the land she had come to call home. Tall, elegant oak and walnut trees seemed to bow under the weight of the sorrow they were witnessing. Only a gentle breeze filtered through them, as if they knew a harsher wind might undo the shattered hearts in attendance.

Then the Solomons could be seen coming, and an ominous

silence settled over the gathering. People moved into place, hands linked with hands. The words of the mercifully short service Brother David preached trembled through Callie's heart. She stood to Ruth Lyons's right, holding her own sorrow at bay by concentrating on the way Ruth conducted herself.

She had marveled more than once at how someone who had lost grandchildren could remain so serene as they huddled in a light drizzle to lay another babe to rest in Jesus' arms.

Callie's heart melted twice; once when she saw Abe's arms tenderly surround his wife, and again when she heard Hannah Grace's soft mewing sounds in the background. She told herself it was due to the grievous nature of what was happening and not because she was in any way jealous of what Abe and Suzannah shared.

First the family, then the others who could bear to do so, threw handfuls of dirt on top of the cradleboard wrapped in several layers of buckskin as they passed by the hole in the earth. All too soon a patch of brown dirt joined the others in the section reserved for female children—set apart by tradition from the men, women, and boys.

Callie viewed through misty eyes the two earlier graves of the Solomon children, noting that grass had refused to grow on them. *There should be flowers,* she thought, renewing an earlier vow to plant something there. As she stared at the plot allotted to Sophie Ruth, all she could think was that the three Solomon children were together in death as they had never been in life. And she had been present at each of their births, unable to change the tragic outcomes. Her heart contracted brutally at the thought.

She started to ease away from Ruth's side when a hand came to rest lightly on her upper arm. She turned, thinking it was Sarah. From the moment she first gazed into the anguish she saw in Joshua's gaze, she was lost.

"Are you all right?" he asked.

She forced a tight smile as she tried to recover from the hurt she saw on his face. She hadn't given a thought to how deeply losing the child might touch him, but the evidence was there for all to see. His normally bright blue eyes were twilight dark, and his characteristic smile was missing. She realized she did not like seeing him without that smile.

"I will be all right," she finally responded. "Why do you ask?"

"Because Sarah mentioned yesterday that you were not feeling well."

"You do not have to worry about me." She glanced around to find her sister chatting with friends. "And Sarah says too many things she should not say."

"That is possible, but I. . ."

"Yes?"

"I worry about you."

Joshua's words surprised her, but with them a strange sense of comfort settled over her tattered soul; she tried to ignore it.

"Well, there is no need. I am fine."

She lightly brushed with her hand at a stray curl that had fallen from her bonnet and wondered silently if he was staring at her red eyes or at the warm color she could feel splashing her cheeks.

"I have done this before, you know," she said.

"Yes, but that does not mean it does not hurt."

At a loss for words, Callie gave him a cursory glance. Joshua's lean frame was attired in a mud-brown jacket and trousers. He had shaved this morning, and a small cut ran under his chin. She had the urge to reach up and smooth her finger across it. She resisted.

Anyone looking at him would see a well-mannered individual with deep worry lines creasing his forehead. He was no longer the stranger he had been a few short weeks ago. With the slight beard he had been growing gone, he somehow looked more mature. And her feelings toward him were not as clear as they had been when he first came to town.

Realizing that he, too, must have suffered through the last few days, Callie almost admitted how desolate she felt. She stopped short. To do so would be to admit to him that she couldn't handle this on her own. And she *could,* she reminded herself; she did not need others to help her make it through tough times.

"Dying is a fact of life," she said. "Especially out here in the wilds where there are so many things that can go wrong."

Joshua arched his eyebrows. "That is true, but there is more to death than dying. And having said that, are you coming to the meeting house for the gathering?"

"The meeting house? I do not think so." If she did, she would end up having to speak with Suzannah, and she was certain she wouldn't be able to think of a thing to say.

"Afraid someone will point at you and say it was all your fault?" Joshua's voice was crisp, hardly like him at all. His words left her shaken.

A rustle of bodies pressed toward them. Callie knew the rest of those gathered there were preparing to leave. She sought her sister and found her immediately, standing with Levi and staring up into his eyes with admiration.

Callie also caught the disgruntled glances of several other women who were looking Sarah's way. Callie tried to catch her sister's eye by waving her hand, but failed. Sarah was oblivious to everyone else.

"She is not doing anything wrong," Joshua interjected. "I suspect she is just trying to be an adult and make others feel better."

"She is my sister and I will thank you to let me tend to her," Callie said.

She instantly regretted her outburst. He had only meant to help, but whenever he was around she seemed unable to think clearly, something she had to work on immediately. She was a grown woman, responsible for the health of over one hundred sixty people. She simply could not allow herself to be bowled over by a good-looking man, regardless of how compassionate and disheartened he looked at the moment.

Joshua bowed. "You are right. I apologize if I violated your duties."

Callie clenched her teeth together. Is that how he saw taking care of family? As a duty? *Then he is no better than Levi,* she thought, recalling Levi's comments about Storm's mother being the one to care for her sick son.

"I need to talk to you," Joshua continued when she failed to speak up.

"Talk? We have nothing to talk about." Callie couldn't keep the sarcasm out of her voice. "There is nothing you could tell me that would make me feel any better." Even as she said the words, she knew they were false.

"What if I said it was about you?"

He put his arm on her elbow and steered her toward the trail, pointing in the direction of the meeting house, where grief was softened and morale bolstered.

"A–about me?" She didn't mean to stammer, but hadn't she been thinking about this very thing lately? "I suppose we could discuss it on the way," she offered. Where were her good intentions now, she asked herself. Why were her knees suddenly resisting holding her up?

"Somehow I do not think that will be a sufficient length of time to say what I have to say, but. . ." Joshua halted as Brother David walked past. They exchanged greetings, and when the elder had departed, he began again.

"I have never been one to turn down the offer of having a fair-haired woman on my arm. Shall we?" He held out an arm to her and motioned down the trail with his other hand.

Callie swallowed hard. Her heart was racing in her chest,

which was hardly an appropriate reaction for someone who had just attended a burial. Oh, why had he chosen now to want to speak with her? Why couldn't he leave her alone? Since he didn't appear about to do so, it was up to her to control herself. She was weak, just as the Bible said.

But didn't the Bible also say, "There hath no temptation taken you but such as is common to man: but God is faithful, who will not suffer you to be tempted above that ye are able; but will with the temptation also make a way to escape, that ye may be able to bear it"? a little voice in her head argued.

What harm could come of her talking with Joshua? He said he planned on enlightening her about some of the things she wanted to know about the orphanage, about herself. Smiling more broadly than she could control and forgetting for the moment how upset she had been at seeing Sarah ogle Levi, Callie slipped her arm naturally through Joshua's. Her fingers lay lightly across his muscular forearm, and she inhaled sharply as he smiled down at her. She had rarely touched Levi in this fashion, but with Joshua it just seemed so natural.

It was not a great distance to the meeting house, a half-mile or so. The grass along the pathway poked green tips through loamy dirt, and here and there a robin searched for food. Crows mingled at the tree line, screeching and performing some sort of ritual walk.

A thunderstorm could have erupted overhead and Callie would have paid it no attention. She could only concentrate on the man beside her. He towered above her, rugged and strong. Other men had walked beside her, but she had never felt as protected as she did with Joshua.

"Brother Joshua," she began as seriously as she could. It was the only way she could maintain her perspective while walking with him.

When he lowered his head to look at her, a warm smile crinkled his blue eyes. "Yes?"

"What brought you here?" She hadn't planned on being so forthright, but she did want to know, if only to satisfy a small portion of her curiosity.

"I have wondered when you would ask."

She thought he might slow down the pace of their walk, but he didn't.

He did, though, reach up with his free hand, remove his hat, and hand it to her. She took it without thinking, watching as he ran his fingers through the locks of thick black hair that chased across his forehead.

"It is a long story, and one I have not shared with many. But since you asked, I will tell you. I fell in love with a woman and planned to marry her. A situation arose and she, well, she was not free to marry me."

Callie pulled back and almost dropped his hat, which she was carrying in her right hand. Why was he confiding in her? She gazed into those blue eyes of his that lately seemed so very capable of upsetting her world.

"That is terrible, but I hardly think you should be telling me this." Did she look as confused as she felt?

"I have no one else to tell," he went on in a whisper. "It is such a relief to finally share it. You see, I carry my love for her in my heart, waiting for the day when she realizes I will never forget her."

Callie pondered his words for a minute, while his fingers tightened a bit on her forearm.

"You make it sound as if she is here, in Schoenbrunn." She flashed a glance at the log cabins of the mission that lay ahead. "That cannot be. No one here has ever mentioned being in love or running from someone."

His eyes narrowed. "Perhaps you are right. Wherever she is, she no longer knows how I feel about her."

"Then you should find her and tell her that instead of hiding out in the wilderness."

Callie had forgotten he was supposed to be talking about her. She marveled he would search so far for a woman he loved.

Joshua smoothed the lines on his forehead. "That was my intent when I began my journey, but certain events have changed my mind."

"Then you have given up your search?" Was she being too inquisitive? She watched him carefully.

He lowered his eyelashes briefly, then shook his head. "I am rethinking my approach. I had planned to confront her and demand we wed immediately." He closed his eyes. "I have decided that will not do at all."

A burst of envy for the woman he loved coursed through Callie. Imagine having a man who would do anything, go anywhere, to find the one woman he wanted above all else.

"I hope you find her one day, Brother Joshua," she said.

Sarah and Levi strolled by, their arms linked lightly and slight looks of astonishment on their faces. Callie recalled that she had not yet spoken with Sarah about Levi's behavior at the spring. She made a mental note to do so as soon as they were alone tonight. The way they were looking at each other made her very uneasy.

As Sarah and Levi followed the trail of tears headed toward the meeting house, Callie turned her thoughts back to Joshua. She admired his determination in the face of adversity, but she did not feel she should tell him that. It seemed too personal, too private. He was holding her arm while they walked and had given her his favorite hat to hold for some strange reason, but she hardly knew him.

Joshua regarded her quizzically. "So do I."

He guided her back onto the path and she watched as he compressed his lips into a tight line. Clearly, their discussion was over and she had not learned a thing about herself. Instead, she had listened to him speak of the fact that he loved someone whom he had come in search of. Someone who had left him? Turned him down? Did not love him? She could hardly pry further. Why did she always find herself in these situations where she couldn't ask what she most wanted to know?

As they walked, Joshua did not take hold of her elbow as he had before. Callie missed his nearness more than she was willing to admit. Just having him touch her had made her feel warm and safe, so different from being with Levi.

She turned her mind back to what he had told her. He had loved, or rather, still loved, a woman who no longer returned that feeling. And he seemed determined to find her again, which meant he would one day leave Schoenbrunn. Had she hurt him, Callie wondered, the woman responsible for the silent mask of pain on his face?

She sighed. It was a tragic tale, but what could she do? Other than the "family" she had established here with the Moravians, she had no basis on which to judge love that occurred between a man and a woman. Early in life, before she was old enough to understand, her parents had cast her away. She had decided in recent years that no one would ever hurt her that way again. Strangely, Callie now found herself questioning that vow.

A shiver ran up her backbone as she remembered what Levi had proclaimed he felt for her. She might be lacking in actual experience, but she was sure that could hardly qualify as love. Other than seeing him with her sister after the burial, she had not seen or spoken with Levi since the episode at the spring. She was convinced he would not pursue her any longer. No, she assured herself, their relationship, if there had ever been one with Levi Lyons, was over.

But why, then, did she feel such a deep sense of loss for Joshua? Because he had come alone to Schoenbrunn? Because he had confided his search for the woman he loved?

It was her nature to care deeply when others were hurting, though she had learned how to keep their pain at a safe distance from her own heart. That way she would survive, just as she had been doing since her accident, and probably as she had been doing all her life but just couldn't remember.

She thought back to what Joshua had entrusted her with as they had stood off the path. The fact that he had given her a quick look at a small part of his past secretly thrilled her. Perhaps others would think it improper that he had confided in her, but since he had brought the issue up, she'd had no choice but to allow him to continue.

After all, he was a man and she had learned that sometimes men did strange things. Yet, there was an emptiness inside her that left her feeling as if they had left things unsaid in that short conversation. And he had not talked about her as he had suggested; he had talked about him. It all made no sense, so she pushed it away, saving it for a later time when she could concentrate.

"So you finally made it," Brother David greeted as they walked around the side of the meeting house.

While Joshua replied automatically, Callie took a last long look at him. He really cut a handsome figure, she decided. She had returned his hat to him, and she admired the way the brim sat low on his brow and cast shadows in the hollows of his cheeks. How blessed the woman was that he loved!

Unbidden, another idea formed before she could stop it. She looked forward to the day when she might find a man who cared enough for her to search through wilderness for her. Surprised at the notion that wedged a twinge of jealousy in a corner of her heart, Callie shook herself. Then as if she knew that was not enough, she issued a quietly stern warning to her heart to stop wishing. Had she not just persuaded Levi that she was not ready to marry?

She caught Brother David staring oddly at her and realized

he must have asked something and was waiting for an answer. Hurriedly, she offered her thanks for the beautiful ceremony he had preached.

"It is the least I can do," he said calmly, making Callie wonder if Joshua had said much the same thing while she had been gathering wool.

"Do you have to help?" Joshua asked as Brother David moved toward the bereaved parents.

Did he want her to stay with him? She was tempted, but her reply was curt. "Usually I hand out coffee and cakes."

Adults congregated in solemn circles and children played in the open area to one side of the meeting house. Tables of baked goods and other food offerings sat along a wall. The sun had come out, burning away the mist that had fallen intermittently throughout the burial service. Its brightness lent a delicate touch to the dismal emotions reflected on the settlers' faces.

Joshua left her to pour coffee, and she watched as he ambled about among the crowd. His height made him an easy target to follow, and she found she could not keep her eyes from straying to him as he stopped and spoke with various groups.

Abe and Suzannah stayed near the worship building, appearing grateful for the attention that helped take their minds off their loss. Callie eyed them discreetly. Every so often, the one holding Hannah Grace would hand the baby to the other, and when their eyes met over the well-bundled infant, there passed an unseen bond.

She had yet to speak with Suzannah. Several times she thought to do so, but each time she held back, frightened of being unable to find words that would convey her despair and her helplessness without further upsetting her friend.

The hollowness inside her was a constant reminder of how she had failed Suzannah—not once, but twice. She could not imagine how Suzannah could ever trust her again.

Suzannah seemed to echo her sentiments, for she rarely glanced in Callie's direction. Finally, the line for coffee tapered off and with nothing else to do, Callie grabbed a piece of jerked turkey and a mug of coffee for herself before joining her sister.

Sarah gestured toward the piece of dry meat in Callie's hand. "I see you are still not eating much."

There was an aloofness about her sister that Callie had not noticed before. Perhaps this was harder on Sarah than she wanted others to know. If that was the case, she would let Sarah work out her emotions on her own.

"I am not hungry right now," she explained. "What do you and MaryBeth have planned for today?"

Sarah appeared to have difficulty swallowing the bite of venison she had just put in her mouth. "Nothing. We are arguing."

Callie sighed. So much happened in her sister's life that Callie did not find out about until afterward. She patted Sarah's arm. "I am sure it will pass. You have had your differences before."

She thought briefly about telling Sarah then about Levi and what he had done the other day, but decided against it. Something of that import was better left for when they were in private.

"It is not me," Sarah returned, dropping her eyes to her food. "We just do not see things the same way anymore."

"You will work it out."

"I am not so sure we will this time," Sarah argued.

Before Callie could ask for an explanation, a loud wail clamored over the muted voices around her. She dropped her food and raced toward the sound, intent on helping in whatever way she could.

Joshua arrived before she could, and she stood back, watching him brush away a young girl's tears who had apparently tripped over a tree root. Joshua ran his forefinger over the scratched skin on the top of her foot.

"You will be fine," he assured the little one.

The child wiped at the side of her face, looked down at her foot as if to see how he had fixed the damage, then beamed a toothless smile up at him. Joshua smiled in return, and the girl pulled her moccasin back on and scampered off toward the children she had been racing with.

He is so good with little ones, Callie thought once the crisis was over and she had moved back to sit beside Sarah. Sarah looked unsettled about something. Callie assumed it was the rift with MaryBeth and said nothing.

The rest of the day passed quickly. Finally, the children collapsed in exhaustion on old deerskins that had been laid on the ground. Adults alternated between eating and talking and watching over the children.

On the spur of the moment, Brother David decided to hold the evening service outside, offering prayers not only for the Solomons, but for the entire settlement. Tomorrow's work was parceled out, good-byes were hugged all around, and the last "Amen" was said as the sun slipped behind the trees at day's end.

☙

Callie put aside the mending she had been working on as Sarah joined her in front of the fireplace, where the snaps and pops of the fire offered a measure of cheer. The rain from the other day had gone, but a chill remained even though it was late May.

"We must talk about your behavior after the funeral the other day, Sarah."

She had truly meant to have this conversation earlier. One illness after another had prevented her from finding the time to do so. The one good thing that had happened in the last two days had been little Storm Killbuck regaining his health. She knew she should congratulate Joshua for that accomplishment, but she hadn't had the time to approach him, either. The two of them had been kept extremely busy.

Sarah was rarely at home lately, slipping in at the last moment to go to sleep. What her sister did around the mission, Callie didn't know. She hoped she had made up with MaryBeth, though. The girls needed each other's companionship, as all humans needed someone in whom they could confide. She had had Suzannah once. It seemed a very long time ago.

"What was wrong with my behavior?" Sarah asked as she tucked her legs beneath her and tugged at her skirt to pull it around her knees like a blanket.

"You were, well. . .it's the way you were carrying on with Levi."

"And what was wrong with that? He was hurting and I was trying to help." Sarah unpinned the braid wrapped around on the back of her head and flipped her strawberry curls until they tumbled down her back.

"You were doing a little more than that!" Callie pointed out.

"You taught me to be considerate of others," Sarah exclaimed. "Are you now telling me I did something wrong even though I saw you doing the same thing with Joshua?"

Callie cleared her throat. "I am not questioning your motives. You are not yet of the age to make weighty decisions such as—"

"Here we go again," Sarah groaned, rolling her eyes.

Callie held up a hand. "Do not get defensive. It is my place to bring you up correctly."

Sarah stared at the fire.

"I am trying to do the best I can," Callie added.

The chill in the room was not only because the fire had not been burning long. Callie knew Sarah disapproved of her speaking this way. She had shown it before, both in words and actions.

A heavy sigh escaped Callie's lips.

"Look, let us not argue," Callie backtracked. "It is the one thing I could not take just now. But in the future, promise me you will behave with more restraint. You know we women are to be seen, not heard."

Sarah turned her head to glare at her, her lips disappearing in a grim line. "Just because you do not know how to have fun, you do not like it when anyone else does, either, do you?"

Callie stiffened at her sister's accusation. She had heard that statement before. "Fun has nothing to do with this. You have got it wrong."

"I am not you, Callie. And I am growing up regardless of how long you try to think of me as your little sister." Sarah tossed her head. "I have done everything you have asked. I came with the Moravians to this godforsaken place. I traveled for weeks, sleeping on cold, hard earth, eating nothing but pemmican and stale bread. Do you know how sick the thought of that stuff makes me?" Sarah grabbed at her throat and acted as if she were choking.

It was not the first time Callie had listened to Sarah rage at the heavens for casting her into this lonely bit of wilderness. She could see an immense struggle taking place in her sister's eyes. She waited, patiently allowing Sarah to work out whatever was tumbling through her mind.

When she spoke, Sarah's words rushed out in an uneven stream. "I even accepted Jesus to keep you from pestering me."

Callie couldn't believe what she had just heard. Pain thudded in her ears. Even as Callie leapt from her seat she was telling herself to stem her reaction. But the anger burning her cheeks and the wave of sickness cresting in her stomach would not fade. And the look in Sarah's eyes said she was serious.

Beneath the enormous burden Sarah had just laid on her, Callie struggled to breathe. Sarah's words thundered in her mind like a horrible storm, shattering her hopes that her sister would grow stronger in Christ.

She grasped the back of the chair. She would not, could not, allow Sarah, who was not yet seventeen, to fall from grace.

"Would you care to explain that for me?" She hated the venomous tone of her voice, but shock prevented her from concentrating on how she spoke.

Sarah shrugged. "It is simple. If God were truly good, He would not do to us what the one you believe in has done."

Sarah's pitiful voice reminded Callie of all the times on the journey to Schoenbrunn that her sister had complained about her lot in life. Callie had passed it off as childish whining, sure it was prompted by the newness of the journey and by the fact that they had just lost the only home they had known.

Hands clenched at her sides, she closed her eyes and prayed for the strength to deal with Sarah's revelation. But while she could shut her eyes and lock out the sight of Sarah sitting in the chair, the phrase *Sarah does not believe,* echoed in her mind.

You are the only person she has to show her the truth, a voice whispered from deep within.

Yes, but how? she argued back.

By showing her love and compassion, by being understanding.

Callie swung away to regain her composure, bidding her tears to subside and her racing heart to slow. What could she say to erase the pain of what Sarah had just confessed? Her fingers dug into the wooden rung of the chair back, and she clung to its surface, holding tightly as if it were the very length of wood that had held her Savior as He breathed His last. When she turned around, ready to speak, Sarah was no longer in the cabin.

Joshua faced the men who had come to the meeting. Weariness pulled their features tight across their high cheekbones, and for those who had been searching all night, their bloodshot eyes testified to their lack of sleep. Joshua himself had not slept in the last three days, but some inner force compelled him to stay awake, as if by doing so he would find the answer to Levi and Sarah's disappearance.

He drew a deep breath and composed his thoughts, which was not easy to do. The images that filled his mind were of Callie and the devastation she must be experiencing because of her sister's actions. A devastation he could only imagine, since she had shut everyone out since that night.

A brief twinge of guilt that he had taken Sarah's side during the incident at the funeral struck him. He shoved it away. Like so many other things, what had happened was history, and he could not change it. What he could change, or at least attempt to, was the way the future looked for his beloved, even if she wanted no part of human contact right now. So, putting aside his own frustration, he straightened his back and motioned around the room.

"This morning some of you brought word of hoofprints along the riverbank north of here," he began. "I know you are thinking we do not know what lies that way, other than more wilderness and French or British soldiers, but it is not our safety at issue here."

He looked around the room, expecting some reaction from the dark-skinned faces. There was none. The glow of the candles hung intermittently along the wall softened the sharp edges of stress on the men looking back at him, but it did not take away the concern on their faces. It was the same concern he was experiencing, but one he tried doubly hard to ignore. If he let himself get muddled up in why he felt it was so important to find Sarah and Levi, he might regret ever coming to Schoenbrunn in the first place.

That, he vowed silently, was something he would never do. Even if nothing came of what he and Callie had once shared, he would relish the fact that he had at least been able to see her again. He turned his mind back to the task at hand.

"We have combed the hillsides, and I think it safe to say that Sarah and Levi, for some unknown reason, have headed north. We have no choice but to follow them."

He stopped, knowing he did not have to remind them that the couple had taken one horse between them, and no one knew what provisions.

"I am going," Joshua announced, his voice echoing off the rafters of the meeting house. "If you are willing to go along, I would appreciate your company."

A barely man-sized voice responded from the back of the room, "I will go."

Joshua turned in the direction of the speaker. Shadow, a young Delaware who had recently given his life to Christ, stood near the back, waving his hand over his head.

"She cannot be allowed to do this to her sister. Or to the rest of her Christian family," the young man added.

Joshua first thought to decline the offer of help from one so young. At fifteen summers, Shadow would have more energy than common sense, but he also had the stamina of youth. He smiled at the boy who was trying to appear mature enough to make such a decision. He was eager, too; but no one except Brother David knew why.

Once Shadow spoke, three others quickly followed suit. After very little discussion, it was decided they would each be outfitted with a horse, a musket, and sufficient dried food for a week's journey. If they had not found the couple by then, they were to return.

"Bring them home safely," Brother David admonished when the men were done planning. "And remember, it is not

our place to serve as judge." The elder had sat quietly
throughout the meeting, putting his implicit trust in Joshua's
ability to handle the details.

"We will bring them home," Shadow retorted. "Whether
they want to come or not." He folded his arms in front of him
as if he dared anyone to dispute him.

Joshua glanced at David, who gave him a slight nod that
said, *Be patient with him and teach him what you know.* He
thought of his father, whom he had not seen in over a year, of
how he had insisted Joshua learn to ride and track, though
he'd had no idea of how Joshua's knowing those things
would ever prove useful. Would he ever see his father again
to thank him for those lessons? With thoughts of family
crowding his mind, he was reminded of the necessity of finding Sarah for Callie.

He dismissed the men to say farewell to their families and
headed toward his own cabin to pack. Strolling up the path,
his thoughts turned to what had happened the night before
last.

He had been treating a patient, so what he knew about the
incident was secondhand, imparted hastily by Brother David
before the first group had ridden out to the south, toward their
sister mission downriver. By that time, the remaining Delawares had broken into small parties with various destinations
in mind.

The elder had been terse while telling him of the disappear-
ances. "I believe they will head toward civilization."

Joshua had agreed with that thinking, but voiced the opinion that he thought Sarah and Levi would avoid any settlement where there would be Delawares present.

"After all," he had pointed out tactfully, "they have left this
mission under the cover of darkness. Why would they seek
the protection of a settlement where they believed people in it
might report their whereabouts to us?"

Other than to stroke his chin thoughtfully, Brother David had given no reply.

The sun glinted on Joshua's face, snapping him out of his reverie. He was surprised to find he was not on his way east toward his house. His footsteps had carried him to Callie's door instead. He stared at it for a moment, trying to reconcile within himself why he had unconsciously come here.

Except for Brother David and those who were ill, she had kept her contact brief with everyone in the mission since the night she discovered her sister missing. She was so intent on hiding away that she rose before dawn to make her morning "sick visits," then returned home before anyone else was up and about.

An indistinct pain clawed at his heart. He should not have promised to avoid telling her more about who he was, Joshua thought irritably. He knew what he had said to her after the burial had been risky, but he had been so sure that if he gave her a hint, she would remember.

He had stopped short of revealing the whole truth only because it would more than likely have destroyed whatever she had begun to build for herself. He would not do that, no matter how much he was tempted to.

How did Callie feel about Levi deserting with her younger sister? The question had plagued him since the moment he had heard about it. Unfortunately, it was one to which he was never likely to discover the answer.

Before he could leave without at least seeing how she was, he rapped at her door. He had spent the last two nights wondering how much of their conversation after the infant's burial Callie had truly heard. The whole time he had been telling her about loving a woman and being unable to wed her, he had hoped she would realize she was the woman he sought. When she had not reacted, he had been forced to admit she might never recall those days they had shared.

Callie opened the door a scant inch, looking as if she had not slept in a week. He wanted to be the balm to her soul she so obviously needed, instead of the source of distress he felt he was for her every time he saw her.

"Yes?" Her voice wavered.

"I have come to check on you." He pushed away words of comfort that were about to burst from his mouth.

"I am fine."

Her response was not strong enough to convince him. Looking out as she was through the tiny space between the door and the frame, he could barely see one side of her face. Tiny drops edged her long lashes, causing a new wave of compassion to well up inside him.

"You do not look it," he answered.

Why didn't he just tell her how beautiful she had once been? How her eyes had sparkled when they found him across the huge room where the orphans ate their meals? How her lips curled up in a smile when she saw him scouting around the grounds for something to do?

She pulled the door open slightly, far enough to gaze up and down the pathway, then stuck a shoulder through the opening. Her gaze hung momentarily on his face as if she were looking for something she knew should be there but wasn't.

"Look," Joshua began, "can you step outside for a moment?"

Hesitation flickered in those brown eyes of hers, but they were a moody brown now, not a laughing brown. Amazingly, she ventured out, sunlight streaming onto the slender column of her throat. Her dress was an older one, and she had not taken any time to tidy her appearance, yet he saw nothing but the beauty she radiated from within. Even the bonnet that appeared as if she had tossed it on her head looked perfect.

"You have news?" There was a scant hint of hope in her voice.

Joshua hated to disappoint her. On top of that, he had to

will himself not to touch her. If he did, it would make leaving harder than the last time he had said good-bye.

"I wish I did."

He felt so inadequate where Callie was concerned. He knew this was no time for regrets. They surfaced anyway. If he had told the whole truth in the beginning, they might be man and wife by now. He would be free to hold her head against his chest and comfort her. Joshua turned away those thoughts before they resulted in some foolish action. Pressing his fingers into his palms, he gazed down at her.

Callie's eyes shifted to the ground. "Then why are you here?"

"To tell you I am going to look for them." He wished there were some way he could erase the heartache she must be feeling.

"Others have done so," she scoffed. "They were unsuccessful. What makes you think you will do any better?"

Joshua didn't blame her for being sour. Life for Callie had been turned inside out. And not for the first time.

"Because no one else has gone so far north," he answered. "There are five of us heading out. I for one am not going to stop until I find them."

"Five?" She seemed to consider the number. "For how long?"

"A week. They will return then."

He held his breath, but she appeared to miss the implication that he might not be with them.

"Godspeed then," she offered, pushing loose curls away from her brow.

He could tell it was taking tremendous effort for her to talk to him. He offered a silent prayer of thanks that she had come out of her cabin for him when she had not for anyone else. Was it meaningful? Had she reached a point where she was beginning to trust him without knowing why?

He ground his teeth together. He was leaving, leaving her behind so he could seek out her runaway sister and the man everyone had thought Callie would marry. Where was the justice in this world? Just as the woman he loved might be realizing there was something significant between them, he was going away.

"Brother David usually says a blessing for those who are going out. Has he done so?" Her voice was so small, yet her words moved him.

"No," he admitted. "Will you come and pray with us then?" It was bold of him to ask, and he held his breath while he waited for her reply.

Beneath the gray lines of her dress, her shoulders tightened. A burst of color on her cheeks made her pale skin look even more delicate.

"I cannot. There will be people there and they. . ." She bit her lip.

Joshua raised his left hand, intent on letting it rest on her shoulders to provide encouragement. Callie stepped back and, seeing her prepare to move, he lifted the hand to the wooden frame of her door and leaned against it instead.

He motioned toward the cabin door with his other hand. "You cannot hide from them forever. They are concerned about you, about what has happened."

"Are they? Or are they gossiping?"

"Surely you know your family better than that?"

Her eyes widened as if she were weighing the word and she had nothing to compare it to. "Family? Oh, my Christian one. Yes, I trust them. It is just that. . ." She straightened her shoulders. "I am not keen on being the object of gos—"

"It is more than gossip, is it not?" Joshua cut in. "People want to help you. That is why we are going out. Does that not prove anything?"

It proves I love you. His plea was silent. The urge to reveal everything was stronger than ever. *If only I could tell you, we would be done with this hedging. And no matter what would happen, it would be worth it to finally say those words to you after so long.*

"It proves you are a fool, going north into unexplored territory," she retorted. Her words faded into nothingness, but there was a spark in her eyes he had not seen since that night at the Solomons' cabin weeks ago. It was there only briefly, and she concealed whatever followed by gazing toward the cemetery.

"Tell me what you are thinking."

He didn't know if saying that made him courageous or foolish. If he could draw her out for a few more minutes, he sensed he would win some sort of battle. But to what end? He was going and not returning until he had information about her sister.

How long that might take was not something Joshua wanted to ponder. Since Callie didn't know who he was, perhaps it was best they end like this. Here, alone, two souls without any apparent bond to each other. Perhaps this was what God had planned after all—to allow him to find Callie, to assure himself she was all right, and then to lead him away before he could hurt her.

A subtle burning pulled at his eyes as he stared at her, willing her to read his mind to see how much he cared for her, had always cared for her, and would continue to do so.

Her eyes locked with his, the power in them such that Joshua knew the moment would be etched in his memory forever. "I am thinking nothing," she replied.

"Your eyes disagree. So, I think, does your heart."

Dare he hope there was a small bit of sadness inside her that he was leaving?

"I am tired," she explained. "You would be too if your sister had run off with someone you had least expected, right after she had. . ."

Heedless of the consequences, Joshua put his hands on her shoulders, feeling every slender muscle beneath them grow rigid.

"Right after what, Callie? What have you not shared with us?" He peered at her, trying to force her to divulge what she knew.

Callie glared back, her mouth quivering. "I have told Brother David what I know about finding Sarah gone," she insisted.

To push further would ruin whatever he had managed to accomplish. He let the weight of his hands rest gently on her shoulders. She didn't pull away. Rather, he thought there might be a slight willingness to share her sorrow with him. He would gladly take that load and anything else, if she would only let him.

"We are departing in two hours. If there is anything we need to know, you must tell us."

"I have already said 'Godspeed.' That is all." She stared at a distant point on the horizon.

His hands fell to his sides. He missed the contact between them immensely. Belatedly, he realized she would think he had come as a friend, not as anything more. He didn't know if that would be enough to sustain him on his trip. But if it was God's will that this is what he would carry with him forever, then he would accept it.

Looking at her now, her shoulders slumped as if the welfare of the world rested on them, he couldn't help but wonder if she was strong enough to go it alone. First the loss of Sophie Ruth, then her sister. How much more could she take?

He checked the sun's position and realized he had just enough time to pack before leaving. Since he couldn't stay and watch over her, he would ask Brother David to keep an eye on Callie and pray for the best. Surely God would keep her safe just a little while longer. . .

❧

Callie heard Joshua's footsteps plodding away from her. She continued staring at the sky, hoping the blue expanse of God's handiwork would help her sort through the emotions warring within her. Crows squawked and cattle lowed nearby, but she was not aware of it—nor of anything else happening in the vicinity.

Why had Joshua come to tell her he was leaving? Did he think that was what she wanted? Had she run him off by her unpleasantness? She had watched him treat ill people with whom she normally would have worked. She had listened patiently to his confession about a love gone wrong. She had conversed with him occasionally, but always came away feeling as if he did not approve of her.

Though tears moistened her eyes, she told herself she did not need Joshua's approval. She had Jesus. That was all she needed.

Yet, if she had been a friend to Joshua as a Christian should, would he still be so eager to leave? Callie wrung her hands together. What had she done? Had she forced Sarah into Levi's arms by being overbearing when all she had meant to do was direct her sister's footsteps in the right direction?

She sobbed. She had not meant to hurt any of them, not Sarah, not Levi, and not Joshua. But they were all gone now. The salty tears that trickled down her cheeks added to her misery. Perhaps Sarah had been right; a loving God would not allow life to be so sour.

Unable to reconcile herself to what the future now held, Callie entered her cabin and flung herself on her bed. She kept telling herself that keeping secret Sarah's admission of her disbelief would not in any way hamper the search party.

Without knowing why, several times she almost caved in and ran to Joshua to inform him of her sister's desertion from God's path. Each time, she quailed at the thought of what he would then think of her. He would question her ability to teach others about God and how to love Jesus. He might also think she was unable to treat those who were sick; and if he returned and decided that, she might find herself out of work at the mission. That would mean she must leave, for she could not bear to stay where she wasn't wanted.

Callie blamed herself for Sarah's departure. She should have identified the change in her sister's behavior, sensed something momentous was about to happen, before it was too late.

That didn't prevent her from grasping the edge of her blanket as she realized how alone she was. A ragged knot formed in the back of her throat, and frustration rippled through her shoulders. Her eyes seemed blistered from the frequent crying she had been doing since she discovered Sarah and Levi missing.

"It is not fair, God. You could have warned me this was going to happen. You have taken everything I ever cared about away from me. Why did You do it?"

Callie didn't stop to consider that she included Joshua as part of the "everything" she cared about. But she did recall some of his last words: "They will return in one week." Did that mean he would not?

nine

The search party gathered by the meeting house to begin their journey. Wives and youngsters held tenaciously to their loved ones, reluctant to let them go. The horses carried saddlebags filled with jerky, corn bread, and dried nuts and berries. Water would be taken from the river they would follow as they headed north.

No one found it easy to leave. Joshua eventually slapped the reins against his horse's neck and pulled on the leather strap of a bridle, and in doing so, assumed command of the group. The horse he rode was the same mount that had brought him to Schoenbrunn a few months earlier.

Noah was a large bay who had seen better days as a plow horse, but Joshua trusted him. The horse tossed his head, and his creamy mane bounced up and down as if he remembered what travel was all about and was anxious to begin.

"Be safe," several people called out while husbands leaned down from their horses to give their wives one last hug.

"Go with God," Brother David encouraged.

Ruth Lyons stood directly behind the elder, leaning against her husband's shoulder. One hand held tightly to her husband's, and the other shaded her eyes from the sun.

"Bring my son back," she said quietly.

Brother David turned and nodded. "They will," he replied. "We have prayed for them."

While the men began their trek, Callie fretted in her cabin. She had wanted to be there to see them off but had been unable to make herself go. She was too afraid of overhearing something that might be said of her, and she didn't want to admit how much it hurt to think of Joshua leaving.

The worry that had coursed through her when he came to tell her he was going had been unlike any emotion she had ever experienced. But somehow she had reached inside herself and found the strength she needed to stand quietly and let him go without saying anything.

Though she couldn't bring her feet to walk through it, she had left her door partway open. Now she could hear the whinny of anxious horses and the calls of the rest of the mission population bidding farewell as the men started out.

She moved quickly to the doorway to watch. Joshua, astride a bulky mount, was easy to spot, and her eyes lingered on him. He raised a hand to wave at the crowd gathered around the meeting house, and discomfort worse than that of riding in a buckboard wagon weighed her down.

As if he sensed what she was contemplating, Joshua turned and glanced toward her cabin. Callie stumbled backward, not realizing the shadows of her home hid her. As she watched, his eyes seemed to tarry on her half-open door, perhaps inviting her to step outside into the open and wave farewell. There was an enormous tug on her heart, and for a moment, her knees weakened.

Nonetheless, as she remembered why he was leaving, her cheeks burned with shame at the memory of having to tell Brother David she had found Sarah missing. And that was just the beginning. It didn't compare to how she felt when they began to suspect Levi had accompanied Sarah.

Callie inhaled sharply. The panic she felt when she had found Sarah gone returned, slicing through her stomach with the claws of a mountain lion. It was made even worse by the fact that she had done nothing but sit in a chair and wait for her sister to return.

Wrapped up in her own disavowal of Sarah's confession, she had thought her sister had run to MaryBeth's and would come back when the two girls had caught up on whatever it was they talked about.

A new wave of helplessness assailed her. Why hadn't she remembered that Sarah had admitted she and MaryBeth had had a disagreement? That Sarah had said she doubted she and the girl would ever work it out? How much of a head start had her failure to act given the couple?

Bitter recriminations stung her eyes while the word "disgrace" echoed in her mind. Sarah had humiliated not only herself but the entire mission by running off with a man and leaving no note of explanation or farewell. Callie tried hard, but at this moment she couldn't see how she could ever forgive Sarah for this. Somehow, she didn't think Sarah wanted her forgiveness anyway.

After all, Callie couldn't help thinking, hadn't Sarah admitted she had confessed Jesus only to pacify her sister? There was no denying Sarah's words. They had poured out of her like water sliding off a cliff. Callie rubbed at her temples where the pounding seemed to hurt the worst.

Where would it end? Would she ever see Sarah again? Or was she destined to remember her as she saw her last—strawberry curls tumbling around her pale face, brown eyes stricken with the deception she had been hiding for who knew how long.

She rose, not bothering to straighten the top of her dress as she usually did after sitting, her weary steps tracing the beginning of a worn trail in the straw on the floor.

"You cannot change history," Brother David had told her shortly after he and his flock had taken her and Sarah into their fold after the flood. "Nor should anyone ever want to, for it makes us who we are today and who we will become tomorrow. If we follow God's path, we can never go wrong."

Remember those words, she told herself. *Cling to them now while my heart is heavy with what Sarah has said and done and the knowledge that Joshua has gone.*

She passed the window and rose up on her tiptoes in the hope of catching a glimpse of the party Joshua led, though they certainly were out of sight by now, having left several minutes ago. Then, realizing the uselessness of her action, she wrung her hands together, hunched her shoulders, and went back to pacing.

≫

Callie's days and nights were oppressed by an agony she could not eradicate from her soul. As she had shortly after Sarah's disappearance, she refused to see anyone, ignoring well-meaning knocks on the door and anxious voices shouting through the wooden planks that had been firmly laced together.

She watched the hours stretch ahead of her, rotating from pink, empty dawn through the day to an even emptier purple night. Bible verses flitted through her mind, but she began to question their truths and promises.

After one particularly harrowing day in which Callie burned her hand on the kettle over the fire and stubbed her toe on a stone barrier put in front of the hearth to help catch stray embers, she collapsed on her bed in tears.

The sound of her door scraping across the wooden frame jolted her. She wiped the fuzziness of tears from her eyes and looked up to find Levi's and Suzannah's mother, Ruth, standing over her. Ruth had her hands settled on her hips and a grim look of determination on a face that was tired and drawn.

"What are you doing?" Callie asked. She was about to demand that Ruth leave her alone so she could continue to wallow in her misery without contaminating anyone else.

"Someone had to tell you, and I figured it might as well be me." Ruth settled into a rocking chair near Callie's bed and gave her a look that warned Callie to listen without interrupting.

"MaryBeth has confessed that she knew Sarah had been

planning something," Ruth announced without any trace of the sunshiny-bright tone she normally used.

Callie absorbed the statement, feeling the slightest glimmer of hope begin to build inside her. She should have thought to ask MaryBeth herself if she knew anything, instead of hiding away from everyone. But the glimmer lasted only a moment. No, she was better off alone. To depend on others was not something she could do. She would face this just as she had learned to face the orphanage and what had happened afterward. Alone.

"How do you know that is not some story MaryBeth made up to get people to quit pestering her?" she contested.

"No one is doing that," Ruth replied. "Perhaps she did not realize Sarah was serious. You know how it is with young people, they sometimes. . ." Ruth's words faded, and a pained expression crossed her face.

Callie had stayed under her covers in her bed. Now she pushed herself up and pulled the blanket up to her chin. "Perhaps that is the problem. I do not understand young people any more than I understand myself."

Ruth covered her face with her hands. "First Suzannah and the baby, now Levi. . ." Sharp agony was apparent in the woman's sobs.

Callie hadn't thought about the fact that Ruth, who had just lost a third granddaughter, had now lost her only son also.

"I am sorry, too, Ruth, but what am I supposed to do? Sarah obviously did not wish to remain here and so she. . ."—she gestured helplessly—"she talked Levi into doing something insane."

Ruth twisted her fingers in the seam that ran alongside her dress. "It might have been Levi's idea. You cannot blame just Sarah."

Callie struggled to hold her tears in. "I think Sarah sees this as a game. She told me that since I had never had fun, I did not know how to let her do so."

Ruth raised her eyebrows. "I am sure she did not mean it. You know how Sarah is, always chattering on and on without meaning much."

"Yes, well, she took us all for fools, did she not?" There was tartness in Callie's tone.

The idea that her sister had deserted her—and with a man, no less—and she had not suspected it, had been eating away at her. She wanted to shout at the heavens in much the same way Sarah had on the trip from Pennsylvania to Schoenbrunn. Instead, she crumpled her hands together in her lap and looked at Ruth.

Ruth's ebony eyes shone bright over her pinched lips, making Callie feel awkward. Here Callie had been feeling sorry for herself, forgetting that the woman across the table had lost so much. Had she no sense of compassion? No, she could feel Ruth's hopelessness as if it were a tangible thing.

"Sarah began acting strangely not too long ago," Callie said without prompting. "Now I see she was leading up to this. I did not press her because she always got so tired of me telling her what to do."

The tears were getting closer. She could feel them filling the lids of her eyes. "All I wanted was to bring her up properly. You understand, do you not?"

And it was all a farce, a little voice inside her head said. *Nothing you did proved to be any good. Sarah is gone!*

Ruth moved to Callie's side. If the woman was desolate, she hid it well. "No one blames you. You did the best you could."

Callie moaned. "But my best was not good enough. She is gone and Levi is with her, and now we have sent men off to explore a part of the wilderness no one knows in order to find them. What if Sarah does not want to be found? What if something happens to her and Levi?"

She didn't say his name out loud, but the concern she had for Joshua was uppermost in her mind, almost pushing away the worry over her sister.

"We must trust God to lead them home."

Callie stiffened. "The whole mission is in an uproar and it is my fault. I would not blame Brother David if he asked me to return to Pennsylvania tomorrow."

Ruth laid a hand on Callie's shoulder and squeezed gently. "It is not in an uproar and you are not leaving. You tend our sick." Ruth's hand trembled, and Callie felt her own weariness mingle with the woman's.

Ruth went on. "Have you forgotten that when we think the world is against us, we must ask God to make it right?"

"So I am allowed to stay because I have skills the mission needs?" Callie asked, deflecting the part about praying. "That is comforting."

She turned tear-drenched eyes toward the woman standing beside her. *A mother would do this,* she thought. *A mother would hold, and hug, and tell me it will be better tomorrow.* But she had no mother or father. She had only substitutes who had their own families and lives to worry about.

Ruth shook her head. "You are staying because we love you. And because you love God. It is His grace that has brought us to this point. The trials we face on earth are designed to make us stronger in the end."

"But Sarah—" Callie began.

"Shhh." Ruth ran her fingers through Callie's hair, arranging the tousled curls into some semblance of order. "Now is not the time to worry. Now is the time to pray."

"God will hate me for saying this, but I cannot. The words will not come." Callie's voice were rife with painful emotion. Without thinking, she threw herself against Ruth's ample frame.

"There, there." Ruth smoothed her hand across Callie's

forehead and looked into her eyes. "God will not desert you. Nor will He desert Levi and Sarah, no matter what they do. He is always there. And there is nothing you or they are going through that He does not understand."

"Do you really believe that?"

A look of surprise flitted across Ruth's face. "Do you think I would have agreed to come to this wilderness if I did not?"

Callie pulled away from Ruth. "Why *did* you come? You and Zeke must have given up a lot to do this." It felt good to think about something else. She was tired of worrying over Sarah—and Joshua.

"There are times in your life when you have to quit looking back at who you were and start looking ahead to who you can become. Zeke and I had our troubles early on, and many times we almost caved in and allowed Satan to control us." She shivered. "How glad I am we did not."

"You mean you almost left Zeke?"

"No. We almost left Jesus."

"What happened?" The question was out before Callie could stop it, but Ruth's arm was around her shoulder and it made her feel more secure than she had in a long time.

Ruth sighed. "You might as well know. Perhaps it will help in some way."

"If you do not want to share, I will understand," Callie said, even though she was very curious.

"Brother David and his flock had camped not too far from our home," Ruth began. "We were young then. Suzannah was a wee babe and Levi was just beginning to kick within."

Ruth's eyes misted over and Callie drew her down onto the bed beside her. Suddenly Callie was the comforter, not the comforted, a role for which she was more experienced.

"We went to one of his fellowship meetings, mainly because he promised a free meal. Nothing was growing in our garden, and hunting did not bring much to our table. We had sold about every piece of furniture and hand-me-down we owned to buy a cow so we had milk."

Callie brushed a speck of straw from Ruth's sleeve. "That is terrible."

"It would have been, had we allowed ourselves to continue." Ruth swallowed hard. "Zeke had taken to traveling around the countryside and snatching stray chickens. I begged him not to, but it meant eating."

"Did you not have relatives who could help you?"

Ruth nodded. "There were kinfolk—lived not too far away as a matter of fact. But they tossed us out when Suzannah was born two months early. Said they knew what we had been doing before we married." Ruth wiped her eyes, then pursed her lips. "We had not. She *was* early, but both sides refused to see us or help us. Said we had made our bed, we could lie in it."

Suzannah's tendency to have her babies early might just run in the family, Callie realized. She shifted on the bed. "Your families disowned you?"

"That is about the size of it."

"How did Brother David make such a difference?" She knew how he had helped her after the orphanage had been destroyed, how his flock had taken her and Sarah in, provided them with shelter and food, and love. And now Sarah had turned her back on that. The memory stabbed afresh in her heart.

"Brother David showed us what God's love is really all about. After we had been to one meeting, we found ourselves going back. The women in the group would take Suzannah so we could listen to the sermons. It was like being home, Callie. No one condemned us for what they thought we had done. They accepted us as we were, no questions asked."

"They loved you. That is what you are saying." The words slipped naturally from Callie's lips. She had known the same kind of acceptance when she had first been introduced to the Moravian flock.

"Yes, but more importantly, they showed us that God loves us and always will."

"Sarah does not think a loving God would let bad things happen," Callie admitted. She could say that much without telling Ruth what else Sarah had said about not believing.

"Suzannah was like that once," Ruth replied. "She did not believe it either."

"Suzannah rebelled? But she is such a strong Christian now."

"You might not recall doing so, but it seems to me that most young folks rebel at least once in their lives. They listen to their minds not to their hearts."

"So you think Sarah might return to God one day?"

"I cannot tell the future, but I do know that since you two joined us, you have given her a solid foundation to build on. It may sound cruel, but if Sarah chooses otherwise, you cannot let that destroy your life. Do you understand me?"

Callie shifted her gaze to the fireplace for a long minute before she looked back at Ruth. "It is the same with Levi, is it not? You brought him up the best you could, but after a point, what he chooses to do is his decision?"

Ruth nodded. "I think there is a young lady you need to visit. MaryBeth has been worried day and night that you will never speak to her again."

"She should not be. It was hardly her fault." Callie was suddenly aware of the truth of that statement. It was not MaryBeth's fault Sarah had run off. There was no one to blame but Sarah and Levi. That included herself, though she was not ready to let go of her guilt yet.

The knowledge didn't change the fact that no matter what she had tried to do, how she had tried to raise her, Sarah was gone. With Levi, who had not so very long ago taken her to the spring and confessed that he loved her! Something was not quite right about the whole thing.

Callie thought back, trying to recreate exactly what Levi had said. Had his actions even then been part of his plan to run away with Sarah? Since that day, he had been strangely detached. On top of losing his niece, Callie supposed she had given him plenty to think about when she spouted off about her not being a trinket to be played with. A lump settled in her stomach. But if she had not pushed him away, he probably wouldn't have taken Sarah and fled. That would mean it *was* her fault.

Ruth touched her elbow and she realized she had been preoccupied. MaryBeth knew something about her sister. She hadn't gotten past the shock of thinking of Levi and Sarah alone together on the trail, but she could not bear to push all thought of her only surviving relative aside.

❧

Callie stood on MaryBeth's doorstep, wishing the last five days had been one of the bad dreams that kept plaguing her.

"Why did you not tell me what Sarah was planning?" She tried not to sound too accusing.

The girl looked at her through eyes as red from crying as her own. "I did not know she really meant it. She mentioned taking a trip a couple of months ago, but how was I supposed to know she was serious?"

That sounded like Sarah, Callie admitted to herself. Her sister had often made comments about wanting to leave the mission, needing to return to Pennsylvania. It would do no good to rail at MaryBeth. The poor child was trembling in her shoes as it was.

Callie inhaled slowly. "MaryBeth. . ." she started, then stopped. The girl was devastated; even in Callie's own emotional state she could see that. "I do not hold it against you. It is. . .I had such hopes you might. . ."

MaryBeth fell toward her, her giant sobs tearing to shreds any piece of Callie's heart that remained unbroken. She embraced MaryBeth, her chin resting on top of MaryBeth's head. If she could not have Sarah, she could at least try to make MaryBeth feel better.

She raised her eyes and looked at the sky. White clouds darted, their wisps looking as if someone had run a giant brush through them. The sun shone with such force, it was almost blinding. Somewhere miles from here, men from the mission were traipsing after her sister and Levi. Joshua was with them. All she had been able to say to him was "Godspeed." She had even refused to go to the meeting house for the farewell prayer. Her heart faltered, and a sinking feeling fell over her.

She thought about the unknown territory her sister and Levi, and Joshua and the search party, were venturing into. Would they make it? All of them? *Any* of them? Despite renegade Indians, overanxious soldiers, hungry wildlife? What would befall them?

MaryBeth's sobs quieted as she leaned against Callie's chest. Callie felt awkward holding her. Sarah had never allowed such closeness. Her pulse drummed away, pushing away her fears for the moment as her own emotions produced wet trails down her cheeks. Despite how she felt about Sarah running away, she desperately hoped that someday she would once again see her sister.

ten

The nightmare woke her again. Three times in the past four nights she had bolted from sleep where she battled dark demons—faceless, voiceless shapes pressing in on her; just hands reaching and grabbing for her.

The heat had been so oppressive, she had found it hard to sleep. And the ever-present dread and anxiety that clung to her as she thought of Sarah did not contribute to a pleasant state of mind, either. Perhaps that is why the terrible dreams had come.

She shivered as she swung her legs to the floor. She had experienced dreams of this sort after the flood and her accident. Then, Brother David had appointed different women to sit with her throughout the nights, to help chase away the screams and horrendous sounds. Why had they returned? It had been well over five years, and she had always associated them with her head injury.

She reached up and fingered the knot located just inside the hairline on the left side of her head. It was the only outward indication of her accident that remained. The bumps and bruises suffered as she was swept along by the raging flood had faded, leaving only a gaping hole in her memory, much as the waters left destruction behind as they receded.

She wished Sarah were here, for then the cabin would be filled with the scent of coffee brewing and stew warming. Sarah had always been first out of bed and had done those tasks.

There will be no more days like that, Callie speculated, as rain began hitting the roof, providing a chilling accompaniment to her morose thoughts.

For a moment she watched the drops cascade down the oiled paper covering the window. The paper had been rubbed with bear fat to help it repel water. Suddenly cold, she grabbed a blanket and tossed it around her shoulders. It was all so depressing—the nightmare and thoughts of Sarah and her deceit.

Her eyes tracked the water sliding down the window covering. She welcomed the rain after the stickiness of the last few days. It meant her rounds of the sick would be delayed, but she had no serious illnesses at the moment to care for.

After Ruth's visit, and her own with MaryBeth, she had resumed working with the mission's ill. Ruth had been right; Brother David was astonished to hear Callie thought she would be asked to leave.

"No one wants you to go," he had exclaimed when she confessed to him that she no longer felt worthy of staying. "You have done nothing to warrant our asking you to depart."

Callie had mumbled that she didn't deserve to be around those who loved God, but the elder would have none of it.

"The events of the last few weeks have depressed you, sister. Give it time. It is just as before, when you recovered from the flood. Your heart knows what is right." He had patted her hand and given her one of his most encouraging smiles, as if that were all that needed to be said on the matter.

It felt good to be wanted, and Callie did so want to believe he was right. But inside she no longer thought she was good enough to be a Christian. After all, she had failed in her effort to teach her sister to live a proper life. She had not been able to save three of the four Solomon children. On top of that, her un-Christian thoughts and words toward Levi proved she was not worthy of God's love.

Perhaps if she were wiser, or older? Callie rubbed at her eyes as tears threaded her lashes. Perhaps if she had had parents who hadn't abandoned her? She whisked the thought away and tried thinking of the garden plot where seedlings stretched their shoots skyward. This was much needed rain for them. She pictured the plants welcoming the refreshing drops.

Thunder suddenly rolled across the village. The room grew dark. She lit a candle and straightened her dress, noticing a small tear in the hem and making a mental note to mend it later.

Thunder cracked again, closer this time, splitting the air with its might. Following it came an eerie roar she could not place.

"I should get fresh water from the spring before the rain becomes too heavy," she murmured to herself.

Half rising from the chair, she heard the rain begin in earnest. Lightning flashed, so close that it brightened the room. She had never liked lightning, and now as twigs snapped on the oak tree beside her cabin, her pulse quickened. In the year they had lived here, there had been few storms that had sounded so ferocious. After one strong storm, Callie had spent the next day picking up leaves and branches. Sarah had helped her, laughing and giggling as they worked.

Sarah is gone, she remembered, the thought throwing a pall over everything. She deserted me just as our parents did. The torment that flowed through her matched the roar of wind outside, and she collapsed into the rocker, oblivious to nature's fury.

❧

Joshua drew his horse to a halt and looked back at the tree-laden terrain they had just climbed. The hill was covered in a soft blanket of early green and led to a valley full of trees that would turn butter yellow and flaming red in the fall. Birds flitted among the treetops. Meandering through the lowland was the river that would lead them back to Schoenbrunn, which they had left six days ago. Or rather, it would lead the rest of the party back.

Noah tossed his head in the air and snorted. They had been together so long, Joshua barely had to guide his mount, which gave him plenty of opportunity to think, to probe his heart and decide what he wanted above all else. Each time, the image of Callie inserted itself in his mind, and just as quickly, he forced it away. To remember the pain in her eyes was worse than not being able to do anything about it. Being on the trail, at least, was a tangible way he could help.

In order to return safely once he left the group, he would need to keep his wits about him. He studied a line of ominous black clouds to the south.

"Looks like we are in for a bad one," he called to the men who had accompanied him. "Let us find shelter and bed down for the night."

"What about the others?" one asked.

Shadow and another had gone ahead to scout for tracks. The plan was for the group to meet up each night. With the storm heading in, they had no choice but to abandon that for now.

"We will catch up with them tomorrow."

He was proud of the distance they had put behind them. Following the muddy red river had not been difficult. Very little brush grew along the banks, allowing them to keep the horses close to the water.

Joshua had not liked agreeing to let Shadow and the other man go. He would have preferred they all stick together, but as Shadow had pointed out, "We can search better if some of us are looking for tracks while the others come along behind, carefully scanning the terrain for Sarah and Levi."

Joshua had nodded, and after a quick prayer in which he beseeched the heavenly Father to guard their footsteps, he had sent them on their way. Each evening, they selected a resting place and waited for Joshua and the others to join them.

The decision to stop now had not been easy. A forbidding tremor worked up his spine, but he passed it off. What choice did he have? The cloud bank was bearing down on them faster than he had realized, and if they didn't hurry, they would be caught out in the open.

The anxious looks on the faces of his fellow searchers said they, too, were worried about not meeting the other two as planned. He gave them a quick smile.

Forks of lightning split the sky and he pulled on Noah's reins. "Let's find cover, boy." He clucked to his mount and Noah picked up his heavy hooves and began to move hurriedly back down the hill.

&

Callie was unaware of the problem until someone pounded on her door. "There has been a storm," came the shout.

Flying down the footpath, her anxiety rose as her eyes traced the storm's destructive path. After sweeping across the east end of the garden, it had torn through a once sturdy pole fence, then pounced upon four cabins, erasing their roofs as easily as children cleaned their slate boards in school.

Branches and leaves were scattered across the greening grass, and chunks of chinking were strewn about. The storm had moved on as rapidly as it arrived, allowing brittle sunshine to illuminate the mission. Fear roiled in her throat, but she thrust her head up, determined to meet this disaster head-on.

"The wounded are at the meeting house," Brother David called from across the clearing where he was already tugging at logs that had been carelessly tossed about by the wind.

She patched minor cuts and bruises, reassured all those she treated that everything would be fine, and wandered back to the entrance. Now that she knew no one had been seriously injured, the sun's glow seemed softer, as if God had lessened the blow.

The worst she had treated had been a bump on Levi's father's head, a wound he sustained by falling over a chair leg in his haste to see the storm's damage. Callie selected a quiet place off to one side from which to watch the activity. Raindrops glittered in the debris-strewn grass and the dusky sun warmed her skin, but there was a hollow feeling in her soul.

The families whose homes had suffered the brunt of the wind huddled together, staring wide-eyed at what was left of their lives. Brother David ran back and forth, seeming to be everywhere at once. A faded gray shirt thrown over his shoulders and a look of fatigue on his face, he hollered directions and paced among the damaged cabins. Someone near Callie called out to him. He hurried over. She watched as he cocked his head and listened to the man explain something.

The elder straightened and looked about him, assessing the situation. Reeling off names, he pointed to the front of one of the cabins.

"See what we can salvage and pile it out of the way."

His gaze met Callie's. He didn't seem at all surprised to see her, but gave her a slight nod of acknowledgment before turning back to his damaged dream.

Callie surveyed the storm's hopscotch method of reclaiming for nature what had come from nature in the first place. The sight left her nauseous, but she forced the queasy feeling away.

A handful of men joined them, their sleek dark hair pulled away from their faces and plaited in tight braids down their backs. They stared together, their jaws tight as they surveyed the scene.

"We must gather whatever we can that is still usable," Brother David said, dismissing the group.

Soon, a pile of usable roof slats stood as a silent tribute to their will to begin anew. Farther away, another pile was growing—it consisted of damaged boards and materials that they would later burn.

While the men worked, the women, led by Ruth Lyons, were inside preparing a meal. Callie joined them. Ruth bustled around, heaping mounds of thin pancakes onto a wooden platter and directing Callie to stir the maple syrup she was warming in a pot over the fire.

The sugary smell of overdone maple filled the cabin. Callie helped collect the sticky sap each year. Some of it was used to make sugar; the rest was boiled down until it became the sweet-tasting liquid in Callie's pot. She took a deep breath, filling her lungs with the pleasing scent.

When there was nothing else to rescue from the damaged homes, the men headed to David's cabin to eat. Sitting out back, eating flatcakes, they discussed how they would reroof the cabins. With full stomachs and aching muscles, they returned to their labors.

Callie checked on the injured she had treated earlier, then went home. She tried to put out of mind the rhythmic thudding of axes that meant restoration of the mission was underway. She realized with a start that Joshua's home had been one of those that had lost its roof.

What would he do now? Where would he stay? Would it matter? Perhaps he would see this as a sign he should not stay at Schoenbrunn. Somehow, the thought filled her with gloom.

Ruth Lyons called out, pulling Callie out of her misery. Without much enthusiasm, Callie motioned for the woman to enter. Strands of silver hair hung from the bun that was usually tightly wound against the back of the older woman's neck, and Ruth's gray eyes were bloodshot.

Callie shifted clothing from a chair to the table to clear a seat. After some small talk, during which both women politely avoided talking about Sarah and Levi, their conversation turned to the storm. Callie recounted the injuries.

"I am so grateful they were not worse than they were," she finished after describing everything she had treated.

Ruth's face brightened. "If it were not for that fool husband of mine, you would have had next to nothing to treat, is that not true?"

Callie agreed, though with little spirit in her words. As if by mutual agreement, they speculated on how long it would take to fix the damaged homes. They determined it would be at least a full week, barring any work on the Sabbath three days hence.

Ruth sighed. "If I know my husband, he will be growling for food again soon." She moved to the door. "Is there anything I can help you with?"

Callie shook her head and watched as Ruth departed.

She was glad Ruth had come by, for now, without anyone to speak with, memories of Joshua ran through her heart. The way he had stood, poised and confident, as he prepared to leave to search for her sister and Levi. The way he had appeared to want to reach out and push away her fears but held back as if he were afraid she would shove him away.

Thinking about him did no good. It would not bring him back, nor would it bring Sarah and Levi back. Despite her best intentions, she continued to see Joshua's laughing blue eyes staring at her. Finally, disgusted with herself, she headed back to the damaged portion of the settlement to again offer her help.

The men had reconstructed a roof frame for one cabin, and with grunts and groans, they were raising it into position. Using a blunt mallet, they forced the notches together where they did not line up just right. A hatchet in someone's hand thudded on the opposite end, chipping off a segment that was too long.

In minutes, the skeleton was in place. All that remained was to fill the gaps with lengths of bark, then add mud and let the sun's heat dry it. Men were sent to the river to collect yellow clay for the chinking. Months of experimenting had proven the yellowish, tacky earth made the best filler.

While the workers were gone, mugs of cold spring water were prepared. When the men returned with the clay, they mixed it with the water and busied themselves spreading the mixture between logs.

Callie contemplated why she had returned to watch the men. *So I can tell Sarah what is going on,* she thought, until she remembered that Sarah was not at the mission, and then she had to wipe at the tears that formed.

Abe Solomon and another man tugged at a log protruding tenaciously from the earth where high winds had planted it. Brother David had a portion of another log wedged under the buried end and was trying to pry the first one out from the hole it was buried in. The only thing they had succeeded in doing was making the mire around the hole slipperier than it had been when they started.

Abe threw his weight against the log. At the same time, the elder pushed down. Abe slipped and fell, splashing mud and bits of bark over all of them. There was a moment of strained silence. All who were watching held their breath. Then the men moved away from the log, holding their sides and laughing.

Before long, a mud-slinging contest had ensued.

"If you cannot beat them, join them," David's baritone rang out. He slung a particularly gooey mass of mud at Abe.

The ruckus brought youngsters, who rapidly realized a game was in progress. Even the most timid child was soon picking up grubby handfuls and heaving them, not caring who they hit. A glob landed on the elder's forehead and dribbled down his eyebrows, giving him the appearance of having raccoon eyes.

A rich peal of laughter rang out. For half an hour the men tossed mud with abandon while the women watched from a safe distance, some with smirks on their lips, others enjoying unrestrained laughter, a rarity for them.

Ruth Lyons launched a double-size handful of mud at her husband. The sight of the demure woman aiming at and hitting her spouse generated a spontaneous roar from those who were not participating. While the men destroyed the once green ground, Callie watched, knowing that once their joy was exhausted, they would turn back to more serious things. Even so, a small chuckle worked its way out of her own mouth.

ॐ

The search party returned two days later, announced by the squeals of children racing through the settlement and accompanied by the grunts of horses who knew they were home. Pushing aside the dress she had been mending, Callie's heart jumped to an unnatural rhythm. Not because she would see Joshua, she told herself as she patted her curls under her bonnet, but because Sarah might be with them.

And if Levi were with her, she would, well, she would find a way to handle that. She'd had a week to think, and after spending the first few nights tossing in her bed, she had come to the conclusion that Levi had taken Sarah with him because Callie had made herself unavailable.

Speeding toward the meeting house, she barely noticed that spring seemed to have fled along with the search party a week ago. The May afternoon was warm, filled with sunshine and trees now in full bloom. She tried to stroll, but it didn't work. She was too eager. She imagined Sarah standing there—humbled and repentant—and her steps quickened.

She found herself rounding the meeting house along with other settlers, her feet barely skimming the ground. The riders were off their mounts, their arms enveloping their families. The horses pawed the ground, giving notice that they, too, expected attention.

As she entered the area where the horses were tethered, she could not help but count the animals.

No! That was the wrong number!

She counted again.

Four.

Her footsteps slowed while shivers danced on her spine. Four horses were too few to have returned with her sister.

Around her the laughter of riders hugging their way through reunions pierced her heart. Her mind refused to accept what she already knew—that she was not looking for Sarah as much as for a lanky frame. But there was no dusty slouch hat topping a head of wavy black hair among those who had returned.

She stood motionless for an eternity before Brother David's arm went around her shoulder in a fatherly way, and he spoke softly, drawing her away from the back of the meeting house as he did.

"The men say Joshua refused to come back."

She wrenched away and covered her ears with her hands.

The elder was not deterred and continued. "It is not what you think. They found tracks. The others knew they were expected, so. . ."

She whipped back to face him.

"But they did not find them," she said. She scowled at her feet and ground a tuft of grass into the dirt with her shoe.

He shook his head as if it were the last thing in the world he wanted to do. "Not yet. That is why Joshua stayed on the trail. He ordered the rest to come back without him."

"Why?"

If he were out there alone, how much danger was he in? At least Sarah had Levi with her.

"He told the others it was something he needed to do," Brother David said.

"By himself? Who does he think he is? He has no help. No food. He could become hurt." She tried not to sound too alarmed, but failed miserably. Her words certainly did not overcome the ominous pang in her stomach.

"He is a man driven by the desire to do the right thing, just as you do, as any of us will do, when faced with a crisis. I admit he is in dangerous country. The reports about the soldiers who seek to control the rivers and streams for furs are not good. Nor are the reports we are hearing about the Indian raids that have begun." He heaved a deep sigh. "We must pray that God will keep Joshua safe."

Prayer! What had that gained her lately? It had not helped Suzannah, nor had it brought her sister or Joshua back. Her stomach clenched.

"I have prayed since the day I discovered Sarah missing," she blurted. Only she knew how many petitions she had whispered.

"Then you have been faithful. Now you must wait for God to reveal His response at the time He chooses."

"What if His answer is that none of them comes back alive?" she asked, barely able to fight off the fear revealed in her eyes.

He did not attempt an answer.

"Where do I go from here?"

"You go nowhere, Callie. This is your home."

Home? It was where she lived, where she prayed, where she hoped. But home? No, she had no home. Home meant family, happiness, hope. She had none of those left.

eleven

The next few weeks passed in a fog. Several travelers arrived from the sister mission downriver, Gnadenhutten, known affectionately as "Ja-nade-den." The German name meant "huts of grace." Most of the Delawares living there had traveled with Brother David on his initial pilgrimage out of Pennsylvania and knew almost everyone at Schoenbrunn.

Like their Moravian brothers and sisters, they were a serious folk, struggling to achieve perfection and looking toward the future with hope. Most had left behind family members and understood the loss Callie endured.

Though the two settlements were separated by a scant few hours of travel, they did not gather together often, and when they did, there was much to catch up on. They shared stories of crop planting, participated in worship services, and helped to clear the land.

The women fussed over Callie, encouraging her without mentioning Sarah's name. Callie didn't bring it up either, for to do so might bring up Joshua's name, which she could not seem to sweep from her thoughts.

Occasional joys reminded Callie that life went on. For example, there was excitement over a new convert baptized into Christ and happiness over the birth of a babe to a family from Gnaden. But even that last was bittersweet, for the birth brought back memories of Joshua assisting Suzannah when they had lost Sophie Ruth.

Callie had cleaned up the red and squalling infant and abruptly handed it to the mother before hastening away, unable to stay because she was not comfortable.

The days seemed hopelessly long without anyone to talk to. Quite often she went to the base of a tree near the cemetery and sat, staring off at the distant rolling hills as if being around those at peace would in some way soothe the ache in her breast, an ache which she realized could be attributed to the fact that she wished to see Joshua one more time, if only to ask him about the orphanage.

One day, she dug scraggly dandelions from a patch growing wild and planted them carefully on the three Solomon graves. Her tears mingled with the clumps of dirt as she patted the earth into place around their roots. Occasionally she looked toward heaven for an answer.

God seemed strangely silent, and she couldn't help but wonder if He had forsaken her much as Sarah had turned from Him.

July was half over when Brother David announced plans for a fellowship day. According to the nineteen rules of conduct each member of their society had agreed on when they established the mission, dancing and drinking spirits were not allowed. The children played games in the newly cleared pasture, and the adults spent the day feasting and moving about among the small groups that formed.

Contentment flowed among the settlers, but their happiness did not improve Callie's outlook. Soon it would be fall, and Callie knew no more of the whereabouts of Joshua, Sarah, and Levi than she had when they left. Unaware, Joshua's name had gradually crept to the forefront of her thoughts. When winter arrived, how would he stay warm and dry? What would he eat? And most of all, she wondered if he ever thought about her.

꙳

Callie had volunteered to watch Storm, the young Delaware who Joshua had helped to save, for a few hours, and she took him to sit under the large oak near her cabin to eat lunch.

Since recovering from the fever that a few months ago threatened his life, Storm had literally grown by leaps and bounds. He was a strong-willed, energetic child with no signs that his illness had weakened him. When he was on the move, Callie had to struggle to keep up with him. While infants continued to frighten her, she was comfortable with those who walked upright, and she enjoyed answering Storm's curious questions.

She hastily prayed a blessing, then handed Storm two slices of bread with creamy apple butter slathered on them. He ate as if he had not yet eaten that day, despite having finished his morning meal just a few hours earlier. When he was finished, he toddled off. Callie leaned back with her palms behind her on the blanket of soft green grass and watched him. Thick black hair dangled around his face as he shouted in glee at the caterpillar he had found crawling up the tree.

"Put it down," Callie admonished gently.

Storm dropped his head until his miniature chin clipped his chest. "My bug."

"It is God's bug. Put it back on the tree so it can climb."

"I climb, too." His eyes shone.

Callie knew he was recalling the walk they had taken yesterday when she had allowed him to totter across a fallen tree. She had kept his hand firmly clasped in hers, but he had thought he had done it all by himself.

She patted her lap. "Sit here and I will tell you a story."

Storm loved stories, for his mother insisted he learn his heritage, even if she could no longer practice what had once been essential ceremonies. Callie smoothed her skirts after she got the child settled. Her fingers traced the features of his sloped jaw, his baby-soft skin tugging at her heart. She wondered what a child of Joshua's would look like.

Heat flamed in her cheeks. What was she doing thinking about Joshua and having children? Children brought heartbreak, if not through dying before they could live, then they might contract a fatal illness or grow up to run off as had her own sister. She would do well to put the idea of what a young version of Joshua might look like out of her mind.

"Do," Storm ordered impatiently.

Thankful for the interruption that pulled her away from dangerous thoughts, Callie began the well-loved tale of how Rabbit got his tail. Storm listened intently, begging her to repeat the part where bits of fluff like feathers fell from the sky and startled Rabbit so much that he began to run around and around.

When she talked about the fluffy stuff falling thicker and deeper, Storm clapped his hands together, though he quieted when the fluff stopped and Rabbit looked around.

As she whispered how Rabbit slept and woke to find himself at the top of a tree, Storm relaxed against her, but she could feel him hold his breath as she talked about a hawk diving toward Rabbit.

"The hawk had huge wings, and though he was after Rabbit, those frightful wings were so big they knocked Rabbit off the branch."

Storm hugged her, bringing a swell of emotion to her heart. By the time she finished the story with Rabbit's ears stretching as branches tugged at them and how his front feet got shorter when he landed on them first, Storm had dozed off.

Callie gently maneuvered him off her lap and onto the blanket, absentmindedly patting his back and feeling his chest rise and fall. Giving in to the peace she was experiencing, she closed her eyes and let the unseasonably warm sun bathe her face.

"You seem to be quite the picture of contentment, Sister Callie." The male voice startled her until she realized it was Abe, Suzannah's husband.

She opened her eyes guiltily. "Uh, yes," she replied,

checking Storm to see if he had slipped away while she had been indulging in reverie.

Abe's weathered face was covered with a fine sheen of dust acquired when he worked with the oxen to dig a new garden patch.

"I heard you have given up teaching the small ones in Sunday lessons," he began. "It is good to see you have not totally given up being with children."

Not too long after losing Sophie Ruth, Callie had begged off working with the toddlers. Did Abe know that since they had lost Sophie Ruth, she was terrified to be around helpless infants?

"I am so sorry. . . ."

Abe held up a hand. "I did not come to get your apology. I came to ask a favor."

"A favor?" What could she do that no one else in the mission could?

He gave her a solemn nod. "I want you to go to Suzannah."

Callie twisted her hands together under her apron so Abe would not see. Go see Suzannah? They had once been the closest of friends, but in recent months Callie had looked for ways to avoid her. The thought of having to look Suzannah in the eye, knowing she had failed her, settled like a boulder in Callie's stomach.

"I do not think that is. . .something I can do." The words strangled her.

"I think it is." There was a subtle plea in his tone.

"But what will I say?" She had thought that over many times without ever finding an answer. She could share, but she could not understand the depth of the other woman's pain. After all, Callie had never had a child and never would. All she had to compare motherhood to were her feelings surrounding the loss of Sarah, something she still struggled with and found easier to ignore than to think about.

"You know her well enough that the words will come naturally. I only ask that you do not tell her you are sorry. Neither of us wants to hear that." He cleared his throat. "And do not ask for our forgiveness. There is nothing to forgive. What happened was God's will. We have made our peace with it, even if we do not fully understand." His jaw tightened momentarily.

Callie knew the longer she postponed going to Suzannah, the harder it would be. Had she really thought she would never speak with Suzannah again? No, she had always understood that she would someday have to but had thought that day far off in the future. The issue was easier to deal with that way.

"So it is time for me to make my peace?" she whispered, the words catching in her throat.

"Yes, Callie. It is time. Suzannah knows the pain you are experiencing. She knows the grief you feel. By sharing, you will help to lighten your load and hers."

Brother David once told her joy and disaster were to be shared. Joy brought smiles, while disaster refined the gold hidden deep within each person. What was the rest of that verse in First Peter? She had forgotten it.

"Perhaps I will go after I have returned Storm to his parents." She glanced at the boy who continued to sleep.

Abe rubbed the side of his neck. "No. Please go now. I will watch him." He looked at Storm, whose thumb had crept to the circle of his mouth, and a brief twinge of pain crossed his face.

Callie cringed. She felt as if she were drowning; but if it was something Abe wanted her to do, she would do it. Somehow.

"Is she in the cabin?" How Callie could even enter that cabin, she didn't know.

"No. At the graves." His shoulders sagged. "Did you plant the flowers?"

Callie nodded.

"I told her that, but it just seemed to go over her head. She has been spending all her time there. I do not know what to do. She is so different than she was before. . .the last time. She will not leave Hannah Grace with anyone. She will not do any sewing. No cooking. Nothing. It is as if she is a hollow shell."

I feel the same way when I think about Joshua, Callie thought, but it was a thought better kept to herself.

"Perhaps she is just tired, Abe." She had not seen Suzannah in a while, since the burial service, actually. How long ago had that been? Days? Weeks? No, four months!

"Every woman is tired for a time after giving birth, but that is not it," Abe said. "It is something else." He threw his hands up in the air. "I do not know how to say it. She is not herself, not the Suzannah I love. Will you go to her?"

Abe looked so sure she would refuse that Callie couldn't turn him down. Hadn't he had enough disappointment in his life lately?

"Of course I will." She rose and dusted off her hands. *But what will I say to her when I see her?* That, too, she kept within her.

twelve

Joshua muttered under his breath as the rope bindings around his wrists were cinched tighter. Raw and burning, his arms were tied behind him and felt as though they would fall off at the shoulders. If they did, it would be a relief.

Two British soldiers had taken him hostage. The one glaring at him now did so through a whiskey-induced haze. How men tolerated what spirits did to their bodies and minds Joshua would never understand.

Though their accent was heavy, he could follow what they said and he did not like the sound of it.

"The man will be proud when we drag this fine catch in," the heavy-set one with a double chin crowed.

Joshua contemplated the use of the word "man." Not once had they given any clue as to who "the man" was. Perhaps it was better he not know.

"Ayc, he will," agreed the lanky, bearded one that had been Joshua's downfall. His piercing eyes glared at Joshua.

The one behind Joshua guffawed and shoved at him. "Get a move on, mate. We have miles to cover before ye rest now."

Turning to his partner, he snorted. "And we thought we would not find anything worth bringing in once we missed that fiery young lass and her man last week."

Ignoring the way the rope cut into his skin, Joshua focused on what they were saying. He had been close to Sarah and Levi for some time, but he was always one settlement behind, a week too late. These men who had captured him had apparently been hoping to waylay Sarah and Levi. What they probably would have done with Sarah, he wouldn't wish on his worst enemy.

Be that as it may, he would have no opportunity to catch up with the couple now. No, all he could do was pray as he had since the day the Moravians had taken Callie away with them: unceasingly.

☙

Callie found Suzannah kneeling in front of the three little mounds of dirt that contained the children she grieved for. A light breeze gusted occasionally, tossing crinkling leaves around as if they were children's playthings.

Normally, Callie enjoyed seeing the colors of autumn. Today she had no interest in her surroundings, not even in the shrieks of children who had just been let out for a break from school. It was simply background noise to her now.

She studied the huddled figure. Suzannah had her legs tucked under her, her hands clasped in prayer. She was back to her normal thin self, though her dress appeared to hang on her more than it ever had before. A hand-woven reed basket sat off to one side. It was Hannah Grace's sleeping place. A swift stab pierced Callie's heart.

"Suzannah?" She muttered the name from a distance, thinking that if she were not heard, she would turn around and leave. The hope was short lived.

Suzannah jerked upright and turned her head, while wiping away crystal drops that were bursting from her eyes. She stared at Callie for a moment, then slowly rose from the soft earth.

"You have come."

It was as if the woman had been waiting for her forever. The words slashed into Callie. Her shoulders shook as she was overcome by guilt for having deserted her best friend when she most needed her.

"Suzannah, I. . ." There were no words. She had searched

for them many months ago when Suzannah's twins were born dead. She had done the same after Sophie Ruth, but she had not found them then, either.

There was a rustle of long skirts and the crackle of dried leaves underfoot. Suzannah flung her arms around Callie's shoulders and emitted tiny sobs, which disappeared into the woven material of Callie's dress.

There was nothing she could do but stand and allow Suzannah her grief. Her own feelings were unsettled right now; and if she spoke, who knew what she might say. Instead, she raised a slender hand to stroke Suzannah's hair.

"Yes, I have come," Callie whispered, feeling even more overwhelmed by guilt than she had imagined. The tremor that passed through Suzannah's body was matched by one of her own.

Suzannah raised her head and put on a brave face. "Do not ever leave me alone again," the woman begged, her hands clasping Callie's and squeezing hard.

Callie returned the pressure, her eyes as bright as her friend's. Without speaking, they strolled to a nearby walnut tree and settled themselves upon the ground. They were not far from Hannah Grace's basket, and Callie felt relieved that Suzannah had not insisted on bringing the sleeping baby with them.

When the significant hush around them seemed too much to bear any longer, she began bravely, "I have been a fool."

She wanted to be honest, to rid herself of the horrible lack of good sense she had exhibited when she deserted Suzannah in her time of need.

Suzannah shook her head. "We have no fools at Schoenbrunn. You did all that you were able to do, and the rest. . ."

But Callie wanted to take the responsibility for her actions. "I came here to tell you. . ." She broke off when she realized she had been about to say she was sorry. It was the one thing

Abe had warned her *not* to say.

"To tell me you are sorry," Suzannah finished for her tightly. She patted Callie's hand. "I know, and we need speak no more of it."

Callie saw there were very few tears in Suzannah's eyes. Enormous relief flowed through her. Without much having been said, they seemed to have breached the gulf between them. Surprisingly, the burning behind her own eyes seemed on the verge of going away for the first time in months.

"Thank you," she said quietly.

Above them, a gaggle of geese announced their impending departure to a warmer climate. The sun silhouetted the fowl as they flew on, two pairs of eyes riveted on them until they became specks in the sky. The sharp scent of burning wood drifted to them from a fire burning where the men were clearing another section of woods.

"I have often wondered what it would be like to be up there," Suzannah mused, still looking at the sky. "To see the world as God sees it. It must be breathtaking."

Callie glanced toward the spot in the sky where the geese had disappeared.

"You would go up there if you could?" For some reason she had never imagined Suzannah having any desire other than to be a wife and mother.

"If I knew I would return to those I love," she confirmed. "Do you not have a dream you wish to see fulfilled more than any other?"

Yes, to see Joshua, Callie thought.

"I do want to see Sarah again, even if she chooses not to stay or to explain why she did what she did," she admitted. No tears pressed at her eyes, and she marveled at how serene she sounded.

"I know. It is as if you have lost a part of yourself and know you will never recapture it." Suzannah's eyes drifted toward the graves, and she studied them with deep concentration. "But beyond that, is there anything else you truly wish to do or have in your future?"

"I suppose that someday when I am old and withered and gray I will wish I had found someone to wed, to share my days with, but there does not seem much hope of that."

She closed her mouth as rapidly as if she had just swallowed a pesky gnat. Where had that come from? She had never thought about regretting she had no one beside her. Why had that answer popped out so readily?

"You do not see what is under your own nose, do you?" Suzannah chuckled. "It is so plain to the rest of the mission, and yet you. . ." she threw Callie a slightly amused look, "you do not see."

"See what?" Callie demanded. What was there to see that was so obvious?

"That Joshua traveled here because he loves you!" the woman exclaimed, her eyes shining as if she had just revealed a well-known secret.

"Where did you come up with that foolhardy notion?" Callie asked with more than shock in her voice. She gave Suzannah a long sideways glance. "I think you have been sitting in the hot sun too long."

Suzannah returned the look, unable to hide the smile flitting across her face. She said nothing, though, and Callie thought about what she had just heard. Silently repeating the words, she found they had latched onto her heart and refused to let go.

Without warning, the conversation she'd had with him after the burial flashed into her mind. He had confessed to her that he was in love with a woman who had met up with circumstances that prevented them from marrying. Was it possible the flood that had taken her memory was the circumstance he referred to? The tiniest flicker of delight shuddered in her soul.

She had naively taken his comments to mean he was searching for that woman, and she had been jealous he would travel alone through dangerous wilderness to find the woman he loved. Even though she knew he had come from the same orphanage she had grown up in, she had never thought his sudden appearance at their mission might be because it was she he was looking for.

Astounded, she searched for answers. Had he truly stayed because of her? Her heart did a quick but strangely comforting bounce. She had no memory of him, no recall of anything he might have said to her before the flood. That was true, but hadn't she felt at ease with him since the very beginning? Hadn't she missed him dreadfully while he had been gone?

Yes, she could not deny it. Since the night he had entered the Solomon cabin and given Suzannah, and herself, a reason to believe that at least one child might survive, Callie had detected something familiar about him.

But she didn't remember him! How could she care deeply for someone she didn't know? She shook her head, willing away the disturbing truth pushing at her. Determined to ignore what was staring her in the face, she turned back to Suzannah, who was watching her as if she followed every twist Callie's mind was taking.

"Will you help me plant more flowers over there?" Suzannah motioned to the graves. "I must add something to what you have already done. It will be my way of saying farewell."

"Flowers will not grow in the winter!" Callie exclaimed. Strange how quickly Suzannah had turned the conversation away from Joshua.

"That is true," Suzannah agreed, "but while I was hurting, you took it upon yourself to try to brighten up my babies' resting places. It is only fitting that I do something to build upon your love. After months of listening to well-meaning speeches by Abe and a hundred others, perhaps it is time to put this behind me and move on."

"You mean. . ."

"I cannot change the past, Callie, no matter how hard I pray, how many nights I fail to sleep, or how many tears I cry. God meant for me to have these children even though He was going to take them away." Suzannah swiped at her cheeks. "Just as we all must face the truth someday, I have found it is time to move on. I will never forget them, but I can try to put the past behind me."

Abe had been worried that Suzannah was at a breaking point from which he could not draw her back. Suzannah was much stronger than most, Callie realized, stronger than she was herself, because she still held to a past she couldn't remember.

"I will help you."

She watched as Suzannah found a small patch of wild clover that still clung to life, though there had been several nights of light frost. Scooping it from the ground with her hands, Suzannah brought it to the graves and divided it into three segments.

"This way they will all share something." She patted the last bits of earth around the wilting green stems.

"There is something missing, though," Callie said. She leaned over and whispered something in Suzannah's ear.

Suzannah grabbed the basket holding Hannah Grace and together they raced toward the river. They returned a short time later, their aprons laden with the small, rounded stones known as "river biscuits."

Callie arranged the stones at the heads of each of the sites.

"There," she said, when tiny semicircles were completed and she had brushed her hands off on her dress. "In case anyone here doubts it, now they are earth's angels as well as heaven's angels."

"You have given them halos!" Suzannah's gratitude was commingled with sobs, but they were not painful ones; they were tinged with acceptance and struck an answering cord deep in Callie.

Peace seemed to flirt with her, and she squeezed Suzannah's hand. No matter what happened in the future, they would share the bond that had sprung anew between them. A tie that bridged yesterday's friendship with tomorrow's hope. She admired Suzannah for having the strength to deal with her loss and move on. She only hoped someday she could do the same.

&

"Did you think I would not see through your plan, Suzannah?"

Callie walked to the far side of the room, crossed her arms in front of her, and waited. When she had hoped to learn to put the pain of the past behind her, she had not meant for it to happen just days after wishing for it.

Suzannah paid no attention to Callie until Hannah was nursing quietly under a blanket. "I only did what I had to do. Otherwise, you would have avoided her for who knows how long."

"So you admit you planned it then?"

"I had to or you would not have learned I trust you with her."

"I thought we settled the trust part at the cemetery?"

"Between you and me, yes, that was taken care of." Suzannah peeked at Hannah and settled back with a smile on her face.

"Quit playing with words, Suzannah. What exactly are you saying?"

"I am telling you it is time to quit regretting what has happened to you."

"I picked her up while you were gone. Is that not what you wanted me to do? Hold her so I would face the demons associated with her birth?"

"Only because she was wailing so loudly that I could hear her over at my mother's house."

That was true. Callie personally thought Hannah's screams had been loud enough to frighten away enemies within a day's travel.

"Then why did you not come running to see what was wrong?"

"You figure it out, Callie. I really do not feel like going through this again."

"You cannot lead me into a conversation and then just drop it! It is not fair."

Callie moved to the table and placed her palms on the top so that she was looking directly at Suzannah.

Suzannah returned her stare. "What is not fair is you acting as if it were a great imposition that I trusted you with my child," she replied.

"Watching Hannah was not an imposition," Callie rebutted.

"It was. . ."

Why was Suzannah being so obstinate?

"What are you looking for? You want me to say it was a joy? A pleasure?"

"Well?"

"Suzannah!"

Why was she having such a hard time admitting the truth?

"It was a. . ."

"Oh, all right," Callie snapped. "It was not so bad. In fact, once she stopped screaming, it was, well, comforting that I had gotten her to stop."

It had been unsettling at first, but one look at that tiny scrunched-up face and she had swooped Hannah into her arms without thinking about the twin that would never enjoy life. Which was exactly what Suzannah had planned.

"I see," Callie murmured, unable to tell Suzannah she sensed she was right.

"I am tired, Callie, but I will say this. God does not judge us by our yesterdays. What He does is watch to see how we learn from what happens to us and what we are going to do with tomorrow."

Callie pondered the words. Suzannah had done the only thing a true friend could—force another to face her pain so that she could move on.

"Someday I will thank you for this, but right now I cannot think of when that will be."

Suzannah smiled, a smile that filled her whole face with joy. "It will be when you hold your own child and know that no matter what happens, you will always love them."

Strange that Suzannah's announcement echoed the very thing Callie's heart seemed to be saying.

thirteen

"Callie? Brother David says you must go to sick room."

Shadow's use of the English language had improved enormously in the last year, but she watched his face as he spoke. Something did not look quite right, though she could not figure out what.

"Who is it this time?" For the last three weeks she had run herself ragged treating one family after another as they suffered through a stomach illness. Just the thought that someone had been sequestered in the cabin set aside for the most serious of illnesses did not bode well.

Shadow shrugged. "Cannot say. He just say you come."

With no idea what to expect, she grabbed her medicine bag, tucked her braid under her bonnet, and donned a cap donated by a handsome raccoon.

Hurrying down the path, she tried to ignore a gust of wind that whipped heavy flakes against the ripening color on her cheeks. Ahead of her, Shadow's lean form seemed to blend into the frozen tapestry of the mission.

As they fought to stand upright in the wind, the thought surfaced that perhaps Sarah had returned and Brother David was granting them privacy. Something clutched at the back of her throat. She didn't realize she had slowed down until Shadow shook her arm.

"Callie? He waits." He motioned down the walkway covered with a lacy blanket of snow.

He? Who? Brother David?

No, if it were Brother David, Shadow would have told her so. Besides, she had seen him this morning at service and he had looked as healthy as ever.

158

Levi?

It must be. Her heart fell to her feet, which felt as if they were encased in blocks of ice. The tears in her eyes were caused by the bitter cold, she told herself, not because she was afraid of who waited for her in the cabin and what he would tell her about her sister.

Then why couldn't she shake the sense of impending doom? A cold chill unrelated to the weather shook her from head to toe. Something had happened to Sarah.

Suzannah's words of a few weeks ago came back to her. "God watches to see what we will do with what we have learned."

What would she do if Levi had brought bad news? How would she deal with that?

Trust in God. He will see you through. She appreciated the fact that the little voice in her head seemed encouraging.

The sound of Shadow pushing the heavy plank door open jerked her to the present, and she searched the interior. Facing away from her on the other side of the room sat a man. Midnight-black curls tugged at the neckline of his jacket. One leg was propped across the knee of the other, and one of his hands twirled a slouch hat crazily around in a small circle.

The jolt to her heart was sufficient to cause her to gasp and drop the bag of herbs she had brought along. Shadow gave her a gentle push from behind, as if he knew she would not make it across the room any other way. With knees as sturdy as a pile of mashed corn, she wobbled toward him, trying to convince her now wildly tumbling heart to behave.

Gracious God, thank you. The words were silent, filled with praise.

She was vaguely aware that Shadow had remained by the door and that the floor was covered with hastily spread dried grass that was disturbed in several places. She barely noticed that there were no tables or shelves, only a few chairs upon one of which sat. . .

"Joshua?"

Had she said his name or simply mouthed it?

She wanted to touch him to assure herself he was real, but she was so stunned to see him that she couldn't move. Her breath was frozen in her chest. A roaring fire cast a soft glow over his silhouette, scattering sparks and ashes as a fine stream of smoke erupted from a log.

He turned partway toward her, his profile made bold by the firelight and strengthened by the time he had been away.

I need strength, Father. I cannot do this alone.

"Calliope. I am glad you could come. Will you sit so we may talk?"

It was not Levi. The relief was immense. Joshua was back! She clasped her hands in front of her apron. Looking at him was just a small pleasure, but if it was all she would get, she wanted it to be a memory that would last the rest of her life. The lake-blue gaze that had upset her world from the beginning was doing the same thing to her now.

"My name is Callie," she said, ignoring the excitement that swirled through her as she moved to sit in the chair across from him. She fiddled with the folds of her skirt, glad she was wearing the dress that was not as faded as the others. Finally, unable to bear not looking at him, she did.

"You are injured!"

"It is good to see you, too."

He is back!

"I, well. . .of course, welcome back." Her eyes traced the set of his mouth. "But you have a bandage on your cheek and Shadow said Brother David asked me to come to the sick room, and the only people we put in here are those who are suffering greatly and—"

"You are concerned about how serious it is. Do not be. It is minor in the overall scheme of things."

Nothing would ever be minor where he was concerned.

"Brother David has granted us time to speak privately, or as privately as we can with Shadow as an escort. There are things I must say, and I will not be deterred from saying them."

He is back!

"Will you listen to me without judging too harshly?"

"What is it about?"

How outrageous I sound!

"Different things, all of which I should have told you before now. But I need to know you will listen."

She nodded, unable to bring herself to say anything else for fear it would be the wrong thing.

"You were Calliope long before you became Callie."

"Calliope?" She pronounced each syllable as slowly as he had.

"Yes."

Her name sounded so good when he said it that she had to suck in her cheeks to prevent her dimples from blooming. *I must remember why he is here,* she warned herself. *He has come to tell me about Sarah. That, and only that.*

"You should be resting," she said.

"After we talk."

He looked as if he had not slept in a week. His clothing was tattered and worn, one sleeve practically falling apart at the seams. It made him look more handsome, but why was she thinking of that? A commotion of unfamiliar feelings twittered through her.

"There will be plenty of time for talk later."

She didn't want to talk. She wanted to sit and absorb the changes in him while he had been gone. Tiny lines radiated from the edges of his eyes. Had they always been there?

"What I have to say will not wait any longer," he insisted.

It was true. Something had happened to Sarah and he had come back to tell her. Callie shook her head to clear the threads of hope that kept crowding her thoughts. She had to focus on what he was saying instead of on what she felt when he looked at her.

"Then tell me and get it over with." She made her voice as flat as possible, which meant she had to ignore her churning heartbeat.

He's about to deliver bad news. Straighten your shoulders. Keep your head up. Put your hands in your lap. Do not let him see how much what he says upsets you.

"I came back because I had no choice."

She was right. Bad news.

"I see."

"You mean you remember me?"

Callie was confused until she recalled Joshua had asked shortly after she had first met him if she remembered him yet.

"No. I thought you meant you came back to tell me something bad happened to Sarah."

"As far as I know, she is fine. She and Levi are married and have returned to the Lord. Without their help, my captors might have succeeded in removing me from o-he-yo permanently."

Callie gave a silent prayer of thanks for Sarah and Levi's spiritual health. It no longer mattered how Levi had behaved toward her, or who had been behind him and Sarah leaving Schoenbrunn. They had asked God's forgiveness. That was what was important. She caught Joshua staring at her as if he expected her to say something. "Were you in danger while you were captured?" *What a ridiculous question!*

"British soldiers thought I was a trapper who had taken their supplies. The only way out I saw was to pray—a lot. Every time they talked, I prayed. Out loud."

Nervous laughter bubbled from her lips, but Callie so liked the fact he had called on his faith for sustenance.

"I had just fallen asleep one night when Sarah waltzed into camp," he said. "She distracted the soldiers while Levi freed me. Of course, it took some doing to get to her away from them. But it was worth it. She risked her life for mine."

Callie gasped. Sarah had risked her life for Joshua! It didn't take away the sting of her sister's abrupt departure from

Schoenbrunn, but it did help ease the guilt Callie had done something wrong in raising Sarah.

"Well, if Sarah is fine, then why are you here?"

Could she be any more blunt? He must wonder if she had any tact at all.

"Because of you."

His eyes held hers prisoner, the intensity so overwhelming that she wondered if that was what was making her pulse pound in her ears.

"Because I felt I at least owed it to you to see if you had recovered from your memory loss," he finished.

She forced her face to remain calm, though it was the last thing she felt like doing. Of course that would be the reason. Suzannah had said he had come here because he loved her. Oh, for the courage to ask if that were true!

"I have not."

"I can help with some of it."

"Please do." She sounded so polite, she thought she might get sick.

He nodded. "You lived in the orphanage my parents ran. From what they tell me, your mother brought you and your year-old sister to us. Father says she meant to come back for you."

Callie was touched that he had thought to tell her that. She had always wondered why she had been abandoned. Joshua made it sound as if something had happened to prevent her mother from returning. That in itself was some comfort. Perhaps she had not been cast off as she had always thought.

"I was luckier than you, for I had my parents, but that did not mean you were not loved."

Joshua related what he recalled of living there while growing up. His mother read nightly to all of them then would hug and kiss each child before they were sent off to bed. As a giant herd, the twenty or so children that lived there would sometimes splash in the creek that ran behind their "home."

Callie sensed immediately it was that creek that had torn apart the only life she had known, but she did not interrupt him. She let him speak, admiring his eyes as they alternated between sadness and elation.

"The flood destroyed everything we owned," he continued. "I did not want to let you go with the Moravians, but my parents insisted I attend medical school. They convinced me it was for the best. I regret that choice." he paused.

Callie hoped he meant what she thought he did.

"One day," Joshua said, "Father insisted everyone should learn to ride. Trouble was, the horses he hired were much too big for the little ones, and most of them ended up standing in the middle of the porch and crying. Your sister was one of them."

He sounded wistful, as if he longed to return to those days.

"You miss him? Your father?"

"Yes, but I have faith I will see him again."

She could not keep her composure from cracking. "You are going home?"

Of course he would go. No strings, no attachments, no tomorrows.

"Perhaps, when the day is right."

When it was warmer, then. She would see him for a few more months. And at least he was honest. She had always known that about him. He had even told her about the woman he loved that did not return his love. She had marveled that his devotion was so strong and that he would wade through a wilderness to find that special woman.

Joshua had to go, Callie realized, so he could search for the missing half of his heart. Wait till she told Suzannah he had not come here for her.

"Why did you not tell me from the start who you were and why you were here?"

He had been tossing the hat around and around his fingers.

Now he laid it to the side. "Call me stubborn, but once I learned you were to marry Levi, I figured there was no hope for me. I had prayed continually for the years we were apart that you would remember who I was. I thought perhaps if you saw me, spoke to me, then you would remember. When it did not appear you were going to, all I wanted was for you to be happy. If that meant stepping aside, I was willing to do so."

"I am not." She smoothed the edge of her apron.

"Not?"

"Not going to marry Levi."

A burden she had been unaware of lifted. That is why she had never been comfortable around Levi. Joshua was the man she loved.

"God is very good." He breathed the words out in a rush.

"You went after him to bring him back to me, did you not?" It didn't hurt as much as she thought it would to ask.

"Partially. But I really went after Sarah. Since she was the only family you had, I knew how important she was to you."

"Thank you."

"That is all you have to say?" He sounded as if he could not believe she did not care more.

Oh, there is more, she thought, *so much more.*

"I owe you a debt of gratitude."

She owed him everything. Even as he rode away, she now knew her heart could love. But only him.

He caught her eyeing his injury.

"Perhaps I will have a dashing scar when it heals."

"If that is what you want." If she could keep her distance, it would not hurt too terribly when he was gone.

"Will it matter to you what it looks like?"

Tremendously.

"Why would it?"

"Some women I have known would be terrified to look at something disfiguring."

She was drawn to it. It was a symbol of all he had done, all he was.

"I thought it was a minor scratch. And looks are not all that make a person who he is," Callie announced. "It is what is in one's heart that matters."

What is in my heart? she asked herself. *Jesus, most importantly. The belief He died for my sins.*

Anything else? Sorrow when I think about what Sarah did. And?

She caved in, finally acknowledging the feeling of utmost comfort that expanded within her when she looked at Joshua.

"So what is in *your* heart?"

Did he have to use that familiar drawl that made her want to shout?

You.

"God."

It was the same answer she had used months ago.

"That is as it should be."

Callie was suddenly glad she had not cast the Lord aside and turned her back on Him. Glad she had kept her faith when life seemed so full of despair.

"Would there be room for someone else?"

"Someone else?"

Did she sound as confused as she felt?

"Yes."

That drawl again! Good thing she was already sitting, or she would have collapsed to the floor.

"As in. . .?"

"Me."

Callie gazed at the strong, willful face she had seen in her dreams for months. They had bantered like this in the beginning. She had enjoyed it then. She was enjoying it now. Immensely.

"You?"

Room? She would always have room for him. They would

be a three-strand cord. The Lord. Joshua. Herself. She regretted that Sarah might never know this kind of happiness.

"You are thinking about your sister, are you not?" Joshua asked softly.

She was amazed at how easily he appeared to read her mind.

"If it is God's will, I would like to see her again. Someday."

She traced the angry red scar that started at the underside of his wrist and ran up toward his elbow.

"When did you get this?"

"When I rescued you from the flood."

She felt woozy, as if it were July instead of December and she had been in the noon heat too long. There was not enough air in that last breath she had taken. It all seemed to be happening too fast, yet it seemed so natural, as if someone with more knowledge and insight than she had was in control and had led them to this point.

๛

Joshua looked at the woman before him. Her high neckline hid the slender length of her throat. Her cheeks radiated a beauty he had remembered in his thoughts throughout his captivity. When he had watched her join the Moravians after the flood, knowing she had no memory of who he was, he'd had to trust that God would bring them together again. And here she was!

She was like a delicate flower, but even the tiniest flowers sometimes thrive in the harshest conditions. Someday he would tell her how much strength he derived from her.

"No matter what you have done, or what you cannot remember, I came here because I care about you."

"Suzannah said you did."

Were those tears in her eyes? Had he put them there?

"She was right. You are not the young woman I fell in love with, but neither am I the young man you cared for then. God taught me a great deal of patience while I learned to deal with losing you the first time. I will not let you go again."

"You mean that?" She sounded incredulous.

"I do. God brought us together again because we had not finished what He began in Pennsylvania. I believe what we have gone through was so that He could make sure we were strong enough to stand up to whatever happens in our future."

"Our future?"

He enjoyed watching her face fill with awe.

"Do you mind if I call you Liope?"

She narrowed her doe-brown eyes.

"That was the special name I had—"

"Yes, you may."

Joshua especially liked the way her brown eyes softened as she gave him that permission. It was as if a fiber of what they had shared before had come to life. No, this was nothing like what they had had before, this was new, and only something designed by God could be so fulfilling.

"Did I call you Josh or Joshua?"

He laughed. "You called me Mr. Johnston. Not once could I convince you to use anything else."

"Oh." She mouthed the word.

"Liope, I do not wish to sound presumptuous, but I have waited for five years for this. There are so many memories I have of us together, of the promises we made to each other, but it does not appear as if you are ever going to recall what we had."

"It does not," she agreed. "But suddenly the past does not matter as much as it used to."

After all this time, could it be this simple? He stretched out a hand and held his breath while she considered what the gesture meant. Slowly, she tangled her fingers with his, palm against palm, heart to heart.

The moment of silence was precious. Their eyes captured and held it so that this special time would always be theirs.

"I have to tell Suzannah thanks," she finally said. She explained what had happened at the cemetery and with Hannah

Grace. "She showed me that if I allow the past to control my future, I will never know what it is like to laugh at life again."

He swallowed hard. Asking should not be this difficult. He had already asked her once to marry him. Those words seemed insufficient for what he wanted to know.

"Liope? Will you laugh with me?"

For a long moment her gaze lingered on his wound, tracing its length as if it signified all they had gone through. Panic rose in his throat. Had he pushed too hard, too fast?

"Absolutely."

She punctuated her answer by bobbing her head. Her bonnet slipped off and her braid cavorted in the air around her shoulders.

It was the answer he had been longing to hear since that fateful night when Brother David had convinced him to let her go. It did not matter that she was crying instead of laughing. Her tears cleansed and healed, preparing her heart for the months and years ahead.

Joshua dipped his head at Shadow, who still stood in a corner, trying to appear uninterested in what was happening between the two but unable to contain the merriment that filled his deep-brown features.

As Joshua unfolded himself from the chair, Liope leaned into his arms. Her head nestled against his chest while his lips brushed the beginning of her plaited curls. He inhaled the scent of winter sunshine that emanated from her golden locks and whispered his gratefulness.

"Father. Thank you for allowing me the privilege of making Liope laugh. I promise to keep her safe until she crosses Your final shore and to always show her that life on this earth is nothing more than a different kind of heaven."

epilogue

Liope brushed at the drops that insisted they had a right to cascade down her cheeks. Every time she looked at the baby who had tried to arrive on the last day of 1775, but missed by a few hours, she cried. They were happy tears, but goodness, would they ever stop?

"Except for you, my Liope, I have never seen anyone so perfect."

Barring the day they had exchanged vows and promised their hearts to one another, Joshua's words sounded more full of delight than she had ever heard. And they started a new round of tears. She smiled first at her husband of twenty-two months, then at the precious gift from God in her arms.

Joshua slid into bed beside her and curled his arm around them. "Sophie Ruth Johnston. I like the way it sounds."

"We did not name her that because of the way it sounds!" Callie exclaimed. "We named her that because—"

"We will always remember the first baby with that name, the one who taught us so much about life," he finished.

"And who taught me to believe in God's plan for my life because He knows what is best for me."

Joshua kissed the tip of her nose, then the baby's cheek. "Correction, my sweet. He knows what is best for us."

author's note

Dear Reader,

Schoenbrunn Mission was the first Christian settlement in Ohio, though the American Revolution led to its collapse after only five years. Located in Eastern Ohio near New Philadelphia, the village has been recreated so visitors can see it much as it was during the 1770's. Markers placed throughout the mission explaining various aspects of life at that time and a museum at the site served as my primary reference material for historical accuracy.

Except for David Zeisberger, all characters in this book are fictional. I cannot guarantee Zeisberger would have said the things I attributed to him, but I'm sure as a missionary, he would have been as understanding and gentle a man as I tried to portray.

For more information on the Shoenbrunn Mission or David Zeisberger, visit the museum in New Philadelphia, Ohio, or read Thunder in the Valley, a book for young readers available in stores or on the following page.

Sincerely,
Tammy Shuttlesworth

There's thunder in the valley!

Will you run. . .or stand firm for Jesus?

The time is the late 1700s, the place, the American frontier. People from Europe are coming to America in greater numbers, pushing the borders of the colonies ever farther west. To greet them are tribes of Native Americans, but they are far from a welcome sight. To the settlers these Indians are wild savages who have no right to learn about Jesus Christ.

David Zeisberger has other ideas. David has a mission: to translate Christian books into Native American languages.

Danger, excitement, and adventure await David Zeisberger as he brings ther Good News to the untamed Ohio wilderness!

224 pages, Paperbound, 5 ½" x 4"

A Letter To Our Readers

Dear Reader:

In order that we might better contribute to your reading enjoyment, we would appreciate your taking a few minutes to respond to the following questions. We welcome your comments and read each form and letter we receive. When completed, please return to the following:

Rebecca Germany, Fiction Editor
Heartsong Presents
PO Box 719
Uhrichsville, Ohio 44683

1. Did you enjoy reading *A Different Kind of Heaven?*
   ❏ Very much. I would like to see more books
      by this author!
   ❏ Moderately
      I would have enjoyed it more if _____

   _____

   _____

2. Are you a member of **Heartsong Presents**? Yes ❏ No ❏
   If no, where did you purchase this book? _____

   _____

3. How would you rate, on a scale from 1 (poor) to 5 (superior), the cover design? _____

4. On a scale from 1 (poor) to 10 (superior), please rate the following elements.

   _____ Heroine   _____ Plot

   _____ Hero   _____ Inspirational theme

   _____ Setting   _____ Secondary characters

5. These characters were special because_____

_____

_____

6. How has this book inspired your life?_____

_____

_____

7. What settings would you like to see covered in future
   Heartsong Presents books?_____

_____

_____

8. What are some inspirational themes you would like to see
   treated in future books?_____

_____

_____

9. Would you be interested in reading other **Heartsong
   Presents** titles?   Yes ❑   No ❑

10. Please check your age range:
    ❑ Under 18   ❑ 18-24   ❑ 25-34
    ❑ 35-45   ❑ 46-55   ❑ Over 55

11. How many hours per week do you read?_____

Name _____

Occupation _____

Address _____

City _____ State _____ Zip _____

What they find on America's vast plains is not what they expected— but it's more than they ever dared to dream.

The wide-open plains of the Dakota Territory form the setting for the lives and loves of four inspiring women making their way in the New World. This captivating volume combines three of bestselling author Lauraine Snelling's novels under one cover, along with a bonus novella.

Journey with these courageous women as they make their homes in the Dakota plains— and allow God to fulfill the desires of their hearts in unexpected ways.

400 pages, Paperbound, 5 ³⁄₁₆" x 8"

Heartsong Presents
Love Stories Are Rated G!

That's for godly, gratifying, and of course, great! If you love a thrilling love story, but don't appreciate the sordidness of some popular paperback romances, **Heartsong Presents** is for you. In fact, **Heartsong Presents** is the *only inspirational romance book club*, the only one featuring love stories where Christian faith is the primary ingredient in a marriage relationship.

Sign up today to receive your first set of four, never before published Christian romances. Send no money now; you will receive a bill with the first shipment. You may cancel at any time without obligation, and if you aren't completely satisfied with any selection, you may return the books for an immediate refund!

Imagine. . .four new romances every four weeks—two historical, two contemporary—with men and women like you who long to meet the one God has chosen as the love of their lives. . .all for the low price of $9.97 postpaid.

To join, simply complete the coupon below and mail to the address provided. **Heartsong Presents** romances are rated G for another reason: They'll arrive *Godspeed!*